Illustrated by the author

Adventures of the ISLANDERS

M.J.Vermeulen

ELSP

First published 2009
by ELSP
16A St John's Road
St Helier
Jersey JE2 3LD

Origination by Seaflower Books, Jersey

Prnted and bound in the UK
on behalf of
JFDi Print Services Ltd.

ISBN 978-1-906641-07 -8

All correspondence and enquiries regarding this book should be addressed to the author:
M.J. Vermeulen at
Rosaire
La Mare
St Andrew's
Guernsey GY6 8XX

The characters in this book are entirely fictitious.
Local names are used but apart from some place names
these bear no relation to places or persons of those names
or any other places or persons existing in Guernsey at any time.

Reference to the book *Prehistoric Monuments of Guernsey*
by J Stevens Cox: Toucan Press, 1982
by kind permission of Toucan Press

This book is dedicated
to my family

CONTENTS

1	Something for Nothing	9
2	The Launching	18
3	Les Fouillages	28
4	Grande Havre	35
5	Esperance	45
6	Kitty goes Sailing	57
7	Herm Island	70
8	Exploring the Bay	85
9	Some Unexpected Discoveries	97
10	The Pirates of Rousse	109
11	Bart's Gran's House	123
12	The Beach	132
13	Onboard at Night	145
14	The Morning After	164
15	The Great Expedition	173
16	The Coastal Path	185
17	The Secret Islands	195
18	Phil to the Rescue	208
	Epilogue	219
	Glossary (The glossary provides additional information on all items in the story marked with an asterisk*)	225

Chapter 1

Something for Nothing

Tom was reading the local paper. He liked to read the E-cycle section, where people could offer unwanted items free of charge to anyone else who might need them.

"Hey, look at this, dad!" he said. "Rowing catamaran, complete with trailer etc., needs some work, free to take away."

"Sounds a bit unusual," said his father. "Are you sure it's free?"

"Yes, it must be," said Tom, "Because it's being E-cycled."

"Is it really, Tom? What's the phone number? Let's have a look in the phone book to see whose it is."

Tom scuttled over with the phone book.

"Yes, it's ... let me see ... ah yes, it's a Mr Mahy at L'islet. Shall we phone him, Tom, and find out a bit more about it?"

"Oh yes please!" said Tom. "Wouldn't that be great, dad. Our own boat, and it needn't cost us a penny!"

Tom's mother laughed. "Like father, like son," she said.

"But don't even think of keeping it here. We just don't have the room."

Tom lived with his mother and father, and sister, Becky, in a small bungalow in the lanes just inland from L'Ancresse Common. He knew mum was right. There was only a small garden, and a driveway only just big enough for dad's car and the van that he used for work.

"Never mind, Tom," said his father. "If it's worth having, we can find somewhere to put it. Maybe down at Rousse."

Tom nodded. He knew the area well, and there was a good bit of hard standing where people kept their boats over winter, putting them back on their moorings in the spring.

"That's not a bad idea, dad, because there's a slipway down there as well, for launching the boat!"

"Okay, Tom, but let's not get carried away. I'd better phone Mr Mahy first, and arrange to have a look at it."

Mr Le Page walked over to the phone and started dialling the number.

"Hello, Mr Mahy? Yes it's Bill Le Page here, phoning about the boat. Hmm yes I see... Well yes of course... yes, yes fair enough ... right then. We'll pop around in about half an hour if that's okay. Right ho we'll see you then. Bye for now."

He put the phone down and looked at Tom. "Well that all sounds pretty good. She's made of marine ply, and she's in reasonable condition, hardly used. Needs a bit of paint and varnish, but he's including various other bits and pieces, lifejackets, anchor and that. Sounds too good to miss really, but he needs her out of the way right now. He hasn't used her for a while, and he needs the space as he's getting the builders in to do some work to his house."

"Yes, but if the boat needs some work, where will you put it?" said Mrs Le Page. She was always the one to think of the practical side of things.

"That's not a problem my love," said her husband. "We'll take her to the vinery*. There's a tow bar on the van, so we'll take her there straight away, if she's any good. Anyway, we'd better get going before somebody else snaps her up. You know what people are like with anything free of charge. See you in a little while, darling. Come on, Tom. Let's get down there quick, before someone else sees the advert."

Mr Mahy's house looked a bit like an old sea captain's house. It was a mixture of red brick and white plaster, and was built in a higgledy-piggledy style with various windows dotted about, some of them round like a porthole, and in the roof was a dormer window leading to a balcony with a flagpole. The flower borders in the front garden were neat and tidy, and in fact the whole place looked immaculate.

"Well goodness knows what the builders are going to do," said Tom's father. "It doesn't look like anything at all needs doing."

Mr Mahy had seen them arrive and he came out to greet them. He was an elderly man wearing grey flannel trousers and a dark blue Guernsey*, and he beckoned them over to the side of the house, where Tom could see the boat. At least it was the shape of a boat which had a tarpaulin over it.

"Give us a hand," said Mr Mahy. "We'll take off the cover so you can get a better view."

The catamaran was a most unusual sort of craft; about fourteen feet long and quite narrow at about four feet six inches wide. The two white painted hulls were each about eight inches wide, and very streamlined. She looked as if she would cut through the water very easily. The decks and sides of the cockpit were varnished, and water-stained in places. The interior needed a clean, and there was some paint peeling off the transoms of the hulls, where they had not quite been covered by the tarpaulin. Apart from that she seemed sound enough. Tom's father smiled and gave him a special look, as if to say "We're definitely taking this home, as quick as we can."

"This is an interesting craft Mr Mahy," he said, "How did you come by her?"

Mr Mahy explained that when he had retired some years ago, he needed a project to keep him occupied. He decided to design and build his own boat.

"She rows pretty well, and she's nice and stable when you climb onboard," he said, "And there's three slabs of foam in each hull so she won't sink, you can be sure of that."

He showed them the other bits and pieces; an anchor and plenty of rope, a pair of oars, two life jackets, a couple of fenders, some paddles, a handheld compass, even a chart and a tidal atlas.

"Pity about the paintwork," he said. "That bad winter a couple of years ago, we had some storms and the tarpaulin got ripped off. I should have got onto it sooner but you know how it is."

"Ah well," said Bill Le Page. "Never mind. We think she's lovely, Mr Mahy. We'll be happy to take her off your hands, and we'll give her a good home. Thank you very much!"

"That's fine," said Mr Mahy. "I'll be sorry to see her go, but we need the space, and I don't think I would have got around to using her again myself. A few too many miles on the clock. And my grandchildren don't seem to be interested."

Tom and his father soon had the boat secure on its trailer and hitched up to the van. By this time Mrs Mahy had come out to meet them, and to make sure Mr Mahy was alright, as she was worried he might be a little bit sad. As they drove off, the old couple stood arm in arm at the front door, and gave them a cheery wave.

Tom kept a careful eye on the boat as they drove along, but it was only a few minutes before they arrived at the vinery.

Bill Le Page's vinery consisted of a piece of land virtually covered by four old glasshouses, with a driveway, a packing shed and a water tower. The glasshouses, or "greenhouses", as they are usually called in Guernsey, had seen better days. Numerous panes of glass were missing or broken, and some of the timbers were starting to go rotten. In places, Bill had put props to keep the greenhouses standing a little longer, but you could see it was only a matter of time before they would need to be taken down.

Until then Bill used the vinery in his spare time, to grow fruit and vegetables and a few flowers for the house, and what was left over was sold on the hedge to passers by. The vinery was also a tremendously useful place for all sorts of things, like storing bits and pieces until you found a use for them, doing some carpentry work in the packing shed, and lighting the occasional bonfire.

Tom loved the vinery. It was tucked away in the lanes about a mile inland from the west coast. Tom found the place had a special atmosphere all of its own. The air smelt of compost, fertilisers, linseed oil putty, timber and paint, petrol and oil, and a myriad other dank and musty aromas. There were stacks of old pots, coiled hoses, pipes and fittings, lengths of timber, old tools and equipment, all gently slumbering in cobwebbed corners. It was so quiet and peaceful. When you arrived you took a deep breath and immediately felt better somehow, just for being there.

Tom watched as his father carefully reversed the boat into a space alongside the packing shed. The space was only just big enough. Then they unhitched the trailer, and had another quick look at their prize.

"It'll be getting dark soon," said his father. "We'd better cover her up and get back home. Your mother will be wondering what's become of us."

Tom couldn't wait to tell his mother the news. On the way back he chattered excitedly to his father about the boat, and Mr and Mrs Mahy, and Rousse, where they intended keeping the boat.

"Well now there's something," said Bill Le Page. "You'll have to give her a name, Tom. I didn't see a name on her, and I forgot to ask Mr Mahy if she had a name."

"Well I don't know," said Tom. "I'll have to think about it, but it could be something to do with cats, as she is a catamaran."

"Hmm yes," said his father. "They often call them something like 'Cool Cat' or 'Tom Cat' or something like that."

They arrived home and parked the van in its usual spot.

"Well, here you are at last," said Tom's mother. "Tea's ready, and I was wondering where you were. So, did you get the boat? Come and tell me all about it."

They washed their hands and took their places at the table, and told her the whole story.

"Well I'm pleased to hear about the lifejackets anyway," she said. "I don't want you doing anything dangerous you know."

Her husband assured her that there was a fair bit to do before they could launch the boat, and he would make sure that everything was as safe as could be, and she was only suitable for use off the beach, and as Tom was a good strong swimmer anyway there was no need to worry.

Tom told his little sister about the boat.

"I think I will sit on the beach and watch," she said.

Becky was not really one for adventure. She would prefer to collect shells, or build sandcastles. That was her idea of adventure.

The next day at breakfast, Tom and his father discussed what needed to be done with the boat. It was arranged that Tom would go to the vinery straight after school and put in a few hours, rubbing down and painting, and his father would pop in when he had finished work, to see how things were going.

"Sorry, Tom," said his father, "But I'm way too busy at the moment to help more than that. Perhaps you could get Ian to help you."

Ian was Tom's best friend, and Tom agreed that he would be just the person to help with the painting, but he would probably like to go out in the boat when it was finished. "Would that be alright, dad?" he asked.

"Certainly," said his father. "If his parents are happy about it that would be a great idea. The holidays are coming up, and honestly Tom, I just don't know if I can take time off. Provided I show you the ropes, I'm sure the two of you will manage fine by yourselves. Ian's a sensible lad. But you will have to stick to the rules, and that's going to be: no more than 50 yards from the shore, and lifejackets on at all times."

"Right," said Tom. "Ian's mum usually drops him off at school, so if I get there in time I can ask them both, and then maybe Ian can help me after school."

And so, after several phone calls between the parents, and assurances from the dads and from the crew that all sorts of safety procedures would be adopted, and after weeks of scrubbing, cleaning, rubbing down, painting and varnishing, under the guidance of Tom's father, the day of launching grew closer.

"Really," said Bill Le Page to Ian's father. "You'd think they were going across the Atlantic. It's only something for paddling about in the bay, and it's far safer than one of those inflatables."

Chapter 2

The Launching

It was the first fine day of the summer holidays when Tom and Ian and Bill Le Page finally arrived down at Rousse in the van, with boat and trailer, all ready for launching. In the nick of time, before the launching ceremony, Tom had finally decided on a name. "I'm going to call her *Kitty Kat*," he said. "*Kitty* for short. I know it sounds a bit funny, but all boats are females, and it's a kind of girl's name, and it's suitable for a small cat, you know…like a catamaran."

It was a gloriously sunny day, with a deep blue sky, and just a few small white clouds floating across it, driven by a gentle breeze.

"Perfect for the launching," said Bill Le Page, as they unhitched the trailer and towed it by hand to the path that led down to the slipway.

"Wouldn't it be great if the Braye du Valle* wasn't filled in!" said Tom. "We could take our boat all the way to St Sampson's Harbour, and then over to Herm*!"

"Never mind Herm," said Bill Le Page. "Fifty yards

from the beach, remember?"

"Yes, dad."

"Yes, Mr Le Page," said Ian.

"Right. Now we're going to walk her down the slip, because the approach is a bit twisty for reversing. Just let her roll down slowly, and keep her pointing in the right direction. You two can do it. I want to see how you get on."

Tom and Ian took a handle each side of the trailer, and carefully guided the boat all the way down the winding path to the water's edge.

"OK," said Bill Le Page. "Now we'll tie that rope to the trailer, and let it roll into the water … that's it … now take the painter, Ian, and hang on to the end. We don't want the boat drifting off by itself! Now Tom, stand up on the trailer, raise the bows and push her off."

The two sailors jumped to it, as instructed, and as the

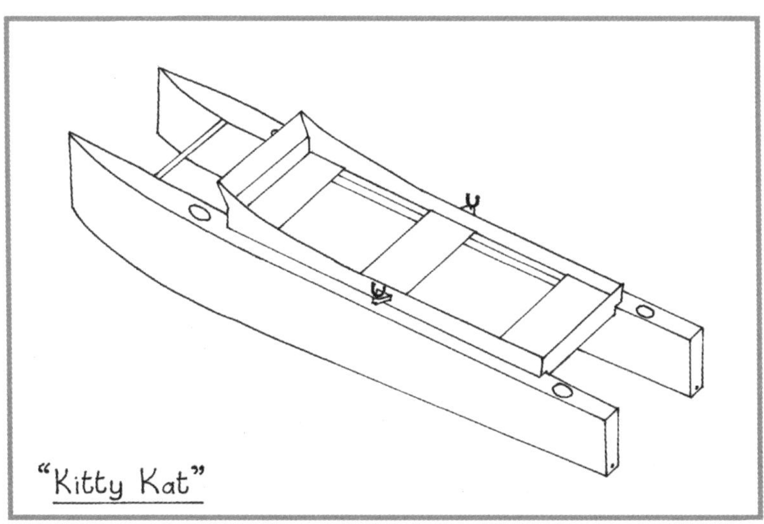
"Kitty Kat"

boat slid into the water Tom shouted: "I name this boat *Kitty Kat*. God bless her, and all who sail in her!"

Tom's father and Ian applauded, and then Bill Le Page hauled up the trailer, while Tom and Ian held onto the boat which was floating happily in the water.

Alongside the slipway an old stone pier jutted out into the bay, used by the fishermen for landing their catch or loading up with equipment. It was also a popular place for swimming or rod and line fishing, and several adults and children had gathered to watch the launching. Tom and Ian had put the fenders out over the port side, so they could bring *Kitty* alongside the pier, where they sat and waited while Tom's father took the trailer up to a safe spot above the high tide mark. The two boys chatted happily while they waited, admiring the boat as she bobbed about on the little waves lapping against the pier.

"Do you think your dad will be coming with us?" asked Ian.

"I don't know," said Tom. "Seems like he's quite happy for us to handle her by ourselves. Doesn't she look great, Ian. I can't wait to see how she goes!"

"Right ho lads," said Bill Le Page as he reached the pier. "She doesn't look so big in the water. I think she'd be a bit crowded with three of us on board, so I'm going to let you two have a go and I shall watch you from the pier. There's one thing you have to watch out for. See those posts sticking out of the water? There's rocks between those posts, so go around, and leave them well to starboard. Now we have to decide who's going to be captain. You can only have one captain on a ship, and his orders must be obeyed."

"Tom has to be captain," said Ian. "It's your boat, after all, Tom."

"Right," said Tom "I'll be captain and dad can be admiral of the fleet. You'll have to be first mate, Ian."

"Now then lads," said the admiral, "We'll just check everything over. Open the inspection hatches, captain, and make sure the bilges are dry."

"Bilges all clear, admiral," said Tom, screwing the hatches back down.

"Lifejackets on? Then climb aboard, lads, and I'll keep her fended off."

The boys clambered aboard. Kitty bobbed a little under their weight, but hardly tipped at all. She felt like a stable platform, just as Mr Mahy had said she would.

"Right ho, mister mate," said Tom. "I'm going to sit in the stern, and you can have first stint at rowing."

"That's fine by me," said Ian.

"No," said Tom "you're supposed to say 'Aye, aye, sir!'"

"Aye, aye, sir!" said Ian.

Tom's father coiled the painter and dropped it onto the front seat. Ian sat on the middle seat, and readied himself with the oars. The fenders were brought onboard.

"Cast off!" said the captain. The admiral gave the boat a gentle shove, and she floated free, away from the pier.

At that moment, as they were cast adrift, Tom was so excited he could hardly speak. Drifting off, away from the shore, in his very own boat. How exciting was that? It was like a dream. He shook his head to make sure he was awake, then took a deep breath, and gave the order.

"Full steam ahead," he said, and Ian gave a pull on the oars.

"Aye, aye, sir," said Ian, and pulled again on the oars, settling down to a steady, if somewhat splashy rhythm.

Kitty gathered speed, and was soon slipping along at a good rate of knots.

"Sorry about the splashing," said Ian. "I haven't rowed for a while. I'd forgotten what hard work it is."

"No, you're doing fine," said Tom. "I'll give you a break in a few minutes."

They set off on their maiden voyage, leaving the posts to starboard as instructed, then heading east into the bay. They passed a line of little rowing boats, used as tenders to the bigger boats moored further out. The tenders were moored fore and aft with pulleys, so they could be pulled into the pebble beach at any state of the tide.

"I wonder if we could moor up like that," said Ian. "It would save all the messing around with the trailer."

"Yes it would," said Tom, "But we'd have to use anti-fouling paint if we left her in the water, and that's really expensive."

Ian had slowed up a bit, and rested for a moment on the oars. It was so quiet and peaceful as they drifted along, enjoying the warmth of the sunshine, and the lovely scene all around them. Looking inland they could see the pale golden sand of the beach they were heading for, the grassy bank above it, and further back a line of windswept pine trees.

"Okay, Tom. Your turn I think," said Ian. They changed

places very carefully to avoid rocking the boat, and as they did so they noticed *Kitty* was still moving slowly through the water, taken along by the breeze.

"I wonder if we could rig up some kind of sail," said Tom. "I don't think it would be too difficult Ian. My dad has loads of wood at the vinery, and rope, and all sorts of pulleys and stuff, and I'm sure my mum could find us an old sheet or something. We could try one like the Vikings had on their longships."

"Yeah, but you'd have to be a bit careful," said Ian. "Too much sail and she might get blown over. A windsurfer sail might be alright, if we could get hold of one."

"Maybe we could try a little sail to start off with," said Tom, "And then, if it wasn't enough we could try a bigger one."

The two sailors chatted away as the boat slowly drifted along, Tom taking a pull on the oars now and then, mainly to avoid some of the boats moored in this part of the bay. There were quite a few to look at, and admire their lines, and discuss which ones they would like to own when they could afford it.

So engrossed were they, in what they were doing, that they had completely forgotten the admiral, who had given up waving at them from the pier, and had decided to drive along the shore to catch them up. The adventurers by now were close to the sandy beach forming the east shore of the bay.

"Ahoy there!" called the admiral. "Come in number nine! Your time is up!"

"OK," called Tom. "We're coming in. Here, Ian, let's take a paddle each and then we can both see where we are going."

So the *Kitty Kat* made her first landing on the beach, and the sailors shipped their paddles and hopped off into the shallow water, hauling the boat as far up as she would go.

"The tide's still coming up at the moment, so you can pull her up as hard as you like," said Bill Le Page. "Now, boys, I think you're getting on fine. I've had a word with Mr Tostevin, and he says you can keep the boat on the laying up area. If you reckon you can manage it, I'll leave you here to row back and trailer her out, while I pop back home for a coffee. I'll be back in about an hour or so."

"That'll be fine, dad," said Tom, "Because Ian and I want to try and fix up a sail of some sort after lunch."

"A sail? Hang on a minute, Tom," said his father. "We'll have to have a chat about that. It might not be as simple as you think. *Kitty* doesn't have a keel or a centre board, and she doesn't have a rudder. How are you going to steer her? Anyway, she's not really meant for sailing. She's too narrow in the beam."

Tom looked a bit disappointed. "But we only want a small sail, dad, just to try it out. Something like the Vikings had on their longships."

"Hmm. Well let me think about it, Tom, but I don't think we should rush into anything."

Ian thought it best not to say anything. This was really between Tom and his father. Anyway he couldn't think of anything useful to say. Tom raised his eyebrows at Ian, and gave one of his looks, as if to say "Parents! Who needs them?"

Bill Le Page set off home for his coffee, and the two sailors sat on the beach for a while, keeping an eye on *Kitty*, as the tide slowly rose and set her afloat again. They had brought the painter up the beach and tied the end to a paddle stuck into the sand, so that she didn't sail off without them.

"I reckon your dad will come up with something," said Ian. "Just leave it for the moment. You know how he loves to invent things. He's sure to come up with something."

"Come on," said Tom after a while, "We'd better be heading back."

They both jumped up, shook off the sand, and trotted down to *Kitty*.

"Shall we paddle back?" said Tom. "She went pretty well with both of us paddling. We can pretend we're savages paddling our war canoe!"

"Ob glob di bobnob!" said Ian, in a suitably savage language, nodding vigorously to indicate his agreement. They clambered onboard and each took a paddle.

"What's savage language for full steam ahead?" asked Tom.

"Hootly bootly bunkum!" shouted Ian.

"Hootly bootly bunkum!" shouted Tom, and they both set too, paddling as fast as they could.

The war canoe fairly flew along, her long thin hulls slapping and bubbling through the water. The wind was against them now, and it was hard work. They were surprised every now and then by a little spray, blowing into the cockpit.

"I think we could do with a bit more decking, just in front of the cockpit, to keep the splashes out," said Ian.

Eventually, two very tired savages paddled the last few yards into the slipway, which thankfully was sheltered under the lee of the pier. The wind by now had increased a little, and the water on the other side of the pier was quite choppy.

"Phew. The sooner we get some sails the better," said Tom.

"You're right there," Ian replied, "But I'm not so sure about a square rig, like the Vikings had. Wouldn't that blow us backwards with the wind against us, like it was on the way back? Maybe we need something else."

"Well, that was a great trip anyway," said Tom. "Just fantastic! Now I'll go and get the trailer, if you want to hang on to *Kitty*."

Ten minutes later, they were pulling the boat and trailer along the last part of the path up from the slipway, when Tom's father arrived just in time to give them a hand for the last stretch over to the laying up area. By now it was nearly half past twelve, and Tom and Ian were ravenous, what with all that exercise and fresh sea air, so they drove back to Tom's house for some lunch.

"I thought you'd be hungry," said Tom's father, "So mum's baked up a big cottage pie for us."

"Cor, that's one of my favourites," said Tom.

"And mine," said Ian.

The adventurers finished off their plates of cottage pie with great relish, and assured Mrs Le Page that hers was easily the best they had ever tasted. After lunch Mr Le Page took his sketch pad from the book shelf and retired to his armchair with a pencil and ruler. Ian smiled and winked at Tom, and they quietly made their way outside, taking a sly peek at the sketch book on the way.

"He's definitely designing something," whispered Tom. "I wonder if it's our sail."

Chapter 3

Les Fouillages

The boys played outside for a while, then told Tom's mother they were going out on their bikes. "Mind you be careful now," she said.

L'Ancresse Common was just a few minutes away from Tom's house. Reaching the end of the lane, they crossed the main road and there they were on the common, which stretched northward for miles into the distance. It was mostly undulating grass and gorse, with a hill towards the north on which a standing stone had been erected to commemorate the Queen's last visit. Bill Le Page thought it was quite funny if that was the best we could do, thousands of years after the stone-age. The common was mainly used as a golf course, for grazing cattle, and occasionally for horse racing. You could just make out the line of the race course, around the edge. The rails had to be put up and taken down again each time there was a meeting. Tom had watched the racing a couple of times, and jolly exciting it was too, with the thundering of hooves as the horses galloped past, the bright colours of the jockeys' silks, and the cracking of their whips as they urged their horses on.

The boys followed the road towards Les Amarreurs, which was a pretty little beach, more or less across the bay from Rousse. Les Amarreurs had its own ancient pier and a few moorings which dried out at low tide. Just before they reached Les Amarreurs they stopped off at the playground to have a go on the swings and the roundabout. They shared the roundabout with a couple of girls who had been using it before they arrived. They hadn't seen the girls before, and asked them if they lived nearby.

"No. We are on holiday," said the taller girl. "My name is Anna Riley, and this is my friend Shani."

She had a strange way of talking, slowly and clearly, so that you somehow had to take notice. She had brown hair, a pale complexion and rosy cheeks, and Tom noticed she had the most incredibly blue eyes. Shani was dark, with black hair and dark brown eyes, and a big friendly smile.

"So what do you think of Guernsey?" said Tom. "Do you like it? Are you having a nice time?"

"Oh yes!" said Shani. "Anna has been here before lots of times, but this is my first time, and I think it's lovely. We live in London. We don't have such lovely beaches there. In fact we don't have any kind of beaches at all!"

"Where are you staying?" asked Tom.

"Usually, we stay with friends of my parents, but seeing as Shani and I need an extra room, we're staying in a hotel over that way," said Anna, pointing south.

"Do you mean the Peninsula?" asked Ian.

"Yes, that's the one."

"That's where we keep our boat, *Kitty Kat*!" said Tom, proudly. "Just across the road from the hotel."

"Wow! Do you really have a boat? What sort of a boat is it?" asked Shani.

"It's a bit unusual. You'd have to see it. Maybe we can show it to you," said Ian.

"It's a catamaran. That's why she's called *Kitty Kat*. We were out in her this morning," said Tom. "We were being savages in our war canoe."

"*Kitty Kat*!" laughed Anna. "That sounds like cat food!"

Tom blushed a little, thinking perhaps his idea for the boat's name had not been so good after all.

"So you were being savages, were you? Do you mean like stone-age men?" asked Anna. "Hmm. You know that's really strange, because I have a feeling about this place." Her deep blue eyes took on a faraway look, and everyone was quiet for a moment, until she spoke again.

"You know these are ancient burial grounds, don't you?"

Tom and Ian thought for a moment.

"Yes," said Ian. "I think there are quite a few stone-age remains around the common, aren't there?"

"Yep. There's a burial site just over there," said Anna, pointing inland.

"Cor. This is really exciting!" said Tom. "Let's go and have a look at it, shall we?"

Just at that moment Anna's mobile phone rang. "Yes mother, we're fine. We're just going for a little walk on the common, then we'll be back. We've met some boys in the playground... Yes okay. Okay then. Right we won't be long. Bye."

The boys looked at her as if she were a creature from outer space. They didn't have mobile phones of their own.

"That was mother," said Anna. "She wants us back on the beach in half an hour, and she would like to meet you guys."

"Come on then, we'd better be quick if we want to look at the burial place," said Tom.

They set off together at a good pace, with Anna leading the way.

"It's not far," she said. "This is a short cut."

They cut across the golf course, and came to a track leading through the gorse. It was a bit like entering a maze, as you couldn't see over the top, and there were little paths leading off from the main track, in various directions. The gorse made a pretty sight, with its bright yellow flowers, but it was best to keep clear of its spikes. Soon they reached a clearing, where they saw a lot of stones laid out in a sort of arrow shape, with some more stones in the middle which looked as if they might once have formed a tomb.

"Oh, I get it," said Ian. "This is the place that's signposted at Lucksall. It's called Les Fouillages."

"Yes. Les Fooyaajs," said Anna, trying to get the pronunciation right. "But we call it the fuselage. It's easier."

On a mound nearby Tom found a plaque giving some information about the site. The writing was quite worn out, and he had some difficulty in making out what it said.

"Hey, look at this! It says it's about 6,500 years old!" said Tom, "And they found 35,000 objects when they excavated it. Surely that can't be right. 35,000!"

The explorers were all suitably impressed. For a moment Anna's eyes again took on that strange faraway look.

"There's something odd about this place," she said. "Something to do with the bay, and the burial site, and the war canoes."

The others looked at one another, not quite understanding, or knowing what to say. It was very quiet and peaceful, as they stood around the stones. The afternoon sun was losing its strength and there was a golden light about the place. In the distance, Tom could see the standing stone which had been put up for the Queen. It felt as if time stood still for a moment, or as if time was all rolled into one. For a short while it almost seemed as if they themselves were stone-age tribesmen, standing in this special place, and it felt as if the act of coming here had somehow bound them together.

It was Anna who broke the spell. "Oh no! Look at the time! I'd better phone the parents, and let them know we're coming."

She made the phone call, and they roused themselves, and made their way as quickly as they could through the gorse and back to the beach, where Anna's parents were waiting by their car.

"Hello you lot!" said Mr Riley. He was a large, jolly

looking gentleman, with a ruddy complexion, silvery hair and a moustache. "Has our daughter been making you late, and getting you into trouble boys? Well don't worry! If she hasn't yet, she will in due course!"

Plans were quickly made to meet up the next day, and then the two girls were whisked away. Tom and Ian walked back to the playground to fetch their bikes, and made their way to Tom's house, where they said goodbye.

"OK Tom. I'll be round at half nine, and we'll go down and show the girls our boat," said Ian.

"Great. See you then!" and they both went their separate ways, thinking what a marvellous day it had been.

That night, Tom lay in bed thinking about all that had happened. If he closed his eyes he could still see the view from his boat of the waves and the sea shore. Then he thought about the girls. Anna was strange and a bit scary, but what beautiful blue eyes she had, and he reckoned she might have some good ideas for adventures. Then there was Shani. She seemed really nice, so jolly and friendly. Then he thought of Ian, and what a good friend he was, and mum and dad, and Becky, as he drifted off to sleep.

Chapter 4

Grande Havre

The next day, the weather was not so good. It started off damp and drizzly, and after breakfast, even though the rain had cleared, the sky was still overcast. Even so, Ian turned up as arranged, and the boys set off on their bikes to meet up with Anna and Shani. Because of the weather, the girls had been wondering whether the boys would show up. It had been difficult to convince Anna's mother that they really needed to stay behind, rather than be taken into the town for some shopping. Anna's father could see they would rather go adventuring, which he would really rather do himself, but he knew this was not a day for parents to be getting in the way. "Come along, dear. I think the girls need some fresh air and exercise, but I'll come with you. You'll be needing a good strong pack horse to carry all that shopping!"

With the parents safely out of the way, the explorers made their way first of all to see *Kitty Kat*.

"Oh! Isn't she lovely!" said Shani, as Ian and Tom proudly rolled back the tarpaulin.

"She's bigger than I expected," said Anna. "I think she would make a very fine war canoe. I can just see the savages in their war paint, paddling her along."

Tom and Ian explained their plans to turn her into a sailing craft, and after further inspection and admiring noises from the girls, they started to discuss what they might do next.

"The parents will be staying in town for lunch," said Anna, "So we have plenty of time to do anything we like."

"I'll tell you what," said Tom. "Why don't we explore the whole bay? If we walk to the headland just up there, we can come back along the shore, and walk all the way around. It's low tide at the moment, and it will be really useful to see where the rocks are."

"Has anyone got a map?" asked Ian. "If we're going to be explorers, we should really have one, and a compass. Or maybe we could make our own map"

" I know where we can get one," said Shani. "There are some by the reception desk at the hotel, and perhaps they might give us some paper to draw one of our own."

"No, it's okay," said Anna. "I have my sketch book in my bag. I'd like to do a bit of sketching if we have time."

"Okay, now what about provisions?" said Tom, who was always mindful of his nutritional needs. "Ian and I have some sandwiches, and chocolate, and some water."

"No, we're fine thank you, Tom," said Shani. "We have some money to buy a snack at one of the kiosks."

"Trading stations you mean," said Ian. "Native trading stations."

"I suppose we could go back and fetch the compass," said Tom, "But it's only one more thing to carry, and I don't really want to go all the way back home just yet."

"No, I think a map will be good enough. We can see which way we're going from the compass point on the map," said Ian.

"Yes, but what about if we get lost in the fog?" said Anna.

"There isn't any fog!" said Tom, "And anyway, if we're just exploring the bay, we could follow the coast back."

Shani popped over the road and collected a map from the hotel, and then they walked in a westerly direction towards the Rousse headland. On the headland was an old granite tower, similar to all the others dotted along Guernsey's coastline, with narrow slit windows through which you could repel the enemy with musket fire. The boys fired their muskets at the girls outside, who made a pretty good job of clutching their mortal wounds and falling dead on the ground with cries of anguish, and the odd giggle. Then they sat on a bench and looked out over the west coast.

"Do you know, there's nothing between here and America. Only the sea... and America's over that way," said Ian. "Must be well over a thousand miles away."

They pondered the vastness of the oceans for a while, and then set off on their journey of exploration of the bay.

They walked past the pier and the moorings at Rousse, past the hotel, and reached a sandy beach. Tom and Ian ran down the steps onto the beach shouting "Yahoo!"

and "Wait for me!" The girls looked at one another with the same pained expression.

"Boys will be boys," Anna sighed, as they followed them down in a more grown- up manner. They eventually caught up with the boys at the far end of the beach and clambered over some boulders up onto a small headland.

"Hey look! There's a German Bunker here," said Ian. "I never knew it was here. And look, right down there at the end there's a little gun emplacement."

They walked around the bunker. Sadly it was covered in graffiti, the metal door appeared to have been forced open, and inside it was full of rubbish.

"Fancy treating an ancient monument like this," said Shani. "It's disgusting."

They found their way onto the top of the bunker, and down to the very end of the point, where the gun emplacement had been cleverly concealed in amongst the rocks. There was a low passage leading to a round hole in the top, where the gun had been positioned. They took turns at crawling in and popping their heads out through the hole to admire the view. You could see the whole of the bay from this point, and looking inland over the lowlands which had once been the Braye du Valle, you could see right through to St Sampson's and even the islands of Herm and Jethou off the east coast. Shani noticed some boats dried out on the far side of the bay. The closest one had a black hull and a funny little white cabin on top, with a chimney poking up through the roof. It was quite a large boat, almost like a little ship. She couldn't be sure, but she thought she had seen smoke drifting up from the chimney.

"Well you're not much good as native scouts," said Anna. "You didn't even know this bunker was here."

"No, we don't usually come around here," said Tom. "It just goes to show how we don't go exploring nearly enough. There must be all sorts of things we could discover!"

"I don't know if I like German bunkers," said Anna. "Certainly not ones in this state anyway. It reminds me of the German Underground Hospital. Mind you, that was fairly clean and tidy when we went there, but it was awfully dark and dingy. I thought it was really spooky."

"Yeah, but it's really interesting though," said Ian. "When you think how they dug out all those tunnels to make a proper hospital."

Shani and Ian were looking at the map.

"This is called Picquerel all around here, and this is Picquerel Point," said Shani, struggling with the pronunciation. "What does that mean Ian? Is it French for something?"

"I don't know," said Ian. "Lots of the place names are Guernsey Patois. It's different to French. Quite often they mean hill, or hummock, or marsh or something like that, just to describe what the place looks like. Or sometimes it tells you what the place was used for."

Anna had made a rough copy of the shape of the bay in her sketch book, and was putting in a dotted line to show where they had been so far. "Right. So this is Picquerel Point," she said, spelling it out as she wrote it on the map. She was tempted to say that native scouts should at least be able to translate their own language, but she thought better of it. She liked Ian and Tom, and she didn't really want to hurt their feelings. "Come on then you lot," she said, "Let's get cracking. We've much further to go."

Tom was really pleased, with one discovery already under his belt. He chuckled to himself as they walked along the path above the beach. It was a well made path, specially made for walkers, and actually a bit too civilised for explorers he thought. Still, when the shoreline became a little less rocky, they could get back onto the beach. The path reached the innermost part of the bay, and turned left, along a strip of common land between the beach and the main road. They found a path leading onto the beach, and sat for a while on the soft dry sand, just above where Tom and Ian had landed in their boat the day before. It seemed like ages ago.

"I do hope this weather clears up," said Tom. "I want to do some more exploring in the boat."

"At least it's not raining, and it's not exactly cold," said Ian. "Maybe we can get out tomorrow. But it's good to have this chance to look at the rocks, Tom. Look at those over there. They must be just below the surface most of the time."

"Yeah. We'll have to keep well clear of those," said Tom, pointing to some rocks which were particularly jagged, and in a position where you might not normally expect them to be. "We'll have to be careful. We don't want to be shipwrecked! But most of the bay doesn't look too bad."

Anna and Ian consulted the map to see if there was anything of interest nearby.

"It looks like this beach is called Pont St Michel, and the road over there is called L'Islet Road," said Anna. "Well that is French. Pont means bridge, and L'Islet means little island, I think. So how could this be a bridge?"

"Well it's not exactly the beach that is a bridge. It's all to do with the Braye du Valle," said Ian, and he went on to explain how the Vale had been a separate island, called St Michel du Valle, and how there was probably a way across at this point when the tide was out. "Probably more of a ford than a bridge," he said.

Anna was getting more and more excited as he explained it all. Her deep blue eyes opened wider and wider.

"You mean in stone age times the sea would have come in here! This would all be under water? That explains it. You see I just have the strangest feelings about this place. It's hard to say what I mean. It kind of feels like the place is just so soaked in history, it's seeping out all over the place. It's like all of the ages, rolling in like waves, and crashing over us. The burial sites. Don't you see?

They must have rowed across to bury their chiefs on a separate island. They probably landed on the beach where we were sitting just the other day! I know I'm right. I can just feel it."

"Well you could be right, I suppose," said Ian, "But don't forget the sea levels may have been different in those days. We were even joined to France at one time, and Guernsey would have been just a great big hill, instead of an island."

"Yes, don't get so excited, Anna. You're always getting too excited," said Shani.

"Well, we all think about things like that from time to time," said Tom. "Perhaps it's just that Anna is more sensitive in that way."

"Maybe I'm wrong, but some things have happened around here which have left a sort of imprint, if you know what I mean," said Anna, calming down. "I just get these wretched feelings from time to time. Sometimes I wish I didn't."

Shani was looking at the black and white boat at the northern end of the beach, tucked in a corner where the shoreline headed out again towards Les Amarreurs. It made a pretty sight. On the shore behind it was a quaint little granite cottage surrounded by trees, and above that the Church of St Michel du Valle, on a hill, with its pointed spire reaching up into the sky.

"There it is again!" she said. "I thought I could see smoke." They all tried to see what she was looking at. "Yes. Over there," she said, pointing at the boat. "Either it's on fire, or there's smoke coming out of its chimney."

"Oh. The old Herm boat?" said Tom. "Yes. You're right there is smoke coming from her, but it doesn't look like she's on fire. Let's go and have a closer look."

They picked themselves up and set off along the beach.

"Do you know?" said Tom, "That boat has been there for years. My dad says she was one of the Dunkirk little ships. Then she was used on the Herm run. But she's been moored there for years now and I've never seen

her go out."

"It's funny really that she's moored so high up the beach," said Ian. "It must be well over half tide before she floats."

"That smoke *is* coming out of the chimney," said Shani, as they got closer. "Somebody must be onboard. Maybe someone lives on her. Maybe it's an old pirate, or a hermit who doesn't want to be disturbed."

"Hmm. Perhaps we'd better go carefully," said Tom. "It's getting near lunchtime, so why don't we walk along the top to the kiosk, oh sorry, I mean trading station, and you girls can get something to eat while we all keep an eye out to see if anyone shows up on deck."

"Good idea, Tom," said Shani. "All this fresh air is making me hungry too!"

Tom smiled at Shani. He liked a girl to have a good appetite.

Chapter 5

Esperance

They walked over to the kiosk, which was clearly a popular place at lunchtime. Several vans and lorries were parked in the carpark, and the drivers were eating their sandwiches, reading newspapers, or enjoying the view out over the bay.

"Ooohh! Look," said Anna. "Bacon rolls!"

"Ooohh yes, I could just do with a bacon roll, and a steaming hot cup of tea," said Tom, forgetting about his sandwiches.

"Yes," said Ian, "And there's Guernsey gache* too!"

"If you like Tom, I'll try your sandwiches, and you can have my bacon roll," said Shani.

"Oh that's really kind of you Shani," said Tom. "Tell you what, let's share, half each."

"Yeah. Let's all share," said Anna. "We'll spread out everything and have a proper picnic."

But before they had a chance to order, they were all rooted to the spot, as Shani, who had been keener than all of them to keep an eye on the old Herm boat, suddenly noticed something moving.

"Shush. Hang on," she said, catching their attention, "There's someone coming out."

Sure enough, a person had appeared on deck. A young blond boy, wearing a Guernsey, a pair of shorts and wellington boots, climbed over the side, down a ladder, and then made his way purposefully up the beach towards the kiosk. He took the path leading up from the beach, and stopped only when his way to the counter was blocked by the explorers.

"Oh, sorry," he said, with a cheerful grin. "Is this the queue for bacon rolls? I'm starving!"

The others laughed at such a friendly greeting.

"Oh no. It's us who are sorry," said Tom. "We've been so busy admiring your boat, and wondering if there was anyone onboard, we haven't got round to ordering yet."

"Yes, we thought you might be an old pirate, or a hermit," said Shani.

"Sorry to disappoint you," said the boy. "Anyway, I was going to buy some lunch and take it back to the boat. I've lit the stove to dry her out a bit, and put the kettle on. If you haven't eaten yet, you're welcome to join me if you like. My name's Bart by the way."

The explorers were almost lost for words at this invitation, but managed to make various polite noises and gestures to confirm that they would be only too pleased to accept.

"That's an unusual name," said Anna, trying to appear nonchalant. "Is it short for something?"

"Don't ask," said Bart. "It's too embarrassing. I don't

know what my parents were thinking about. And please don't mention the Simpsons!" he pleaded.

Shani couldn't help giggling, but Bart just gave her a smile and a wink.

"Come on," said Bart. "The tide's coming up and she'll soon be afloat. If you want to come onboard we'd better get going."

"But how will we get back?" asked Anna.

"Oh don't worry about that. See, over there. We've a dinghy on a pulley between the boat and the shore, so we can get up and down any time," Bart assured her.

They quickly ordered their provisions and trudged down over the beach, over the seaweed at the high tide mark, the soft dry sand becoming firmer and wet underfoot as they approached the boat. "*Esperance*" was the name on her stern. She was soundly built in timber, about 40 feet long. From a distance she had looked quite smart in her black and white, but close up you could see that the paintwork was peeling and clearly she was an ancient old lady who had seen better days.

The tide was coming up fast, and was already lapping around her bows.

"Come on then, up you go," said Bart. "We've no time to spare."

They climbed up a sturdy ladder, tied near the stern. Tom was first on board. He could hardly contain his excitement. What an adventure! Here he was, standing on the deck of one of the little ships of Dunkirk. What tales this ship could tell of daring rescues from the Normandy beaches. He could picture the soldiers wading out from the shore, battle weary, wounded and desperate, bullets and shells exploding all around them. "Right. Let's have those bacon rolls, while they're still warm," said Bart.

They shared out the rolls and tucked in. They hadn't realised how completely ravenous they were. The rolls were quickly devoured, followed by the sandwiches Ian and Tom had brought, followed by thick slabs of buttered gache, and washed down with Tom and Ian's water and some lemonade bought from the kiosk. Tom and Ian kept their chocolate as emergency rations for later.

As they ate, they took in their surroundings. There was a vast area of deck space, and a forepeak cabin with a padlocked door.

"There's deck chairs and sunbeds in there," said Bart. "We can rig up an awning later on, and make ourselves comfortable."

Bart showed them the main cabin, with its tiny portholes and funny curved roof. It looked quite small from the outside, but was surprisingly roomy inside. There were a couple of steps leading down, cupboards and a sink to the right, the stove opposite the door, and, on the left, two separate bunks, one on each side. The cabin was really warm and cosy with the stove lit, and an old black kettle bubbling gently on the hob.

"She's starting to float," Tom called from up on deck, peering over the side. "I'm sure I felt her move."

Sure enough, the tide was coming up fast. The water around the boat was now about three feet deep, and they could all feel a very gentle bumping, as she floated, then touched, then floated again.

"It's not a very high tide today, but she will be afloat now for about five hours or so," said Bart. "Well, Ian and Tom, I think the sun is finally coming out. Could you give me a hand do you think, to put up the awning?"

"Aye, aye, sir!" said Ian and Tom together. This was Bart's ship, and while they were on board, they were the crew and Bart was the captain.

Bart unlocked the forepeak cabin, and hauled out an old canvas tarpaulin, which they rigged up over a rope stretched between both masts, to form a tent over about half of the deck. They tied the outer edges of the tarpaulin to the bulwarks.

"That's a fine old bit of canvas that. It'll last for years," said Bart. "Better than this plastic rubbish."

Then they brought out the deck chairs and sun beds, and the whole crew tried these out while Bart went to fetch the tea.

"This is wonderful. I feel like a princess," said Anna, as Bart served up the tea. "Yes. Like Cleopatra on the Nile," said Shani.

"This is the life," said Ian.

"A life on the ocean wave!" sang Tom.

"Yes, the only trouble is we're not getting our exploring done," said Ian.

"Oh, I am sorry," said Bart. "You should have said. I didn't realise you had other things to do. How thoughtless of me. I do apologise."

"No, no, it's not your fault, Bart," said Ian. "No, don't worry about it. We can do our exploring anytime. Anyway, this is much better than exploring. We're having a lovely time, and thank you so much for inviting us."

"Yes, thank you, Bart," chorused the others.

"So what are you exploring then?" asked Bart, and they told him about their visit to the stone-age burial site, and their idea of exploring the whole bay, and their visit to Rousse Tower, and the discovery of the bunker at Picquerel Point. Anna told him about the strange feelings she had about the area and its history. Bart listened very attentively and nodded.

"Yes, you're right. This area is full of history. Even this boat. Do you know she was one of the Dunkirk little ships?"

"Yes, my dad told me," said Tom. "But how did she end up here in Grande Havre? Wasn't she used as a Herm ferry?"

"They started using bigger boats on the Herm run, and when they sold her off my grandpa bought her. He was going to do trips around the bay, but then everyone started going to Spain for their holidays. So he put the cabin on, and since then we've just used her as a sort of floating beach house, for picnics, swimming, bird watching, you know... that sort of thing. And we keep the dinghy here as her tender, and for a bit of sailing, and pottering about. So she's still pretty useful really. Anyway, we would never get rid of her. We've had her so long, life wouldn't be the same without her."

"There's nothing half so nice as simply messing about in boats!" Tom quoted.

"You're right there Tom," said Bart. " Now, those

dolmens you were talking about. You know there's one just down the road at Sandy Hook? And there are quite a few on the common."

They chatted away, and the time passed quickly. Tom and Ian told Bart about their boat Kitty Kat.

"We might come and visit you one high tide!" said Tom.

"I can see we're going to have a great time!" laughed Bart. "I was expecting things to be really quiet, but now there's so much to do, I don't know how we'll fit it all in. You see, I have to get over to France next week, to visit my father, and then I have to get back home. I'm over staying with my gran at the moment."

Ian and Tom were impressed at Bart's globe trotting life style.

"Look," said Anna. "We need to get organised. Bart isn't the only one having to leave. We only have a week left, and part of that we have to spend with the parents. They want to take us over to Herm on the next fine day, which they reckon could be tomorrow. So we'll have to plan everything we want to do, and see if we can fit it in."

"Absolutely," said Ian.

"Do we have to get organised?" said Tom. "I would rather take each day as it comes."

"So would I," said Shani.

"I don't think we can, Tom. There just isn't time," said Anna. "Look, how about if we each say one thing we want to do. That will be one, two, three, four, five things. Then at least that will be a start," said Anna.

"OK," said Bart. "I would like to have a look at some of the dolmens. In fact I think my gran might have a book somewhere about them, which I can try and get hold of. It might tell us where they are. No, hang on a minute. I would like to do that, but I also want to do some sailing. Yes, put me down for sailing. Oh, and I sometimes like to sleep onboard. Wouldn't it be great if all of us could camp out on the boat overnight!"

"That's three things," said Anna. "But it would be great to sleep onboard, if the parents would let us. Anyway, I'll put you down for sailing, Bart, and I will put my name down for exploring the dolmens. Now Shani, what about you?"

"I would like to go swimming, and spend some more time on the beach, and camp out under the stars. That would be so romantic!" she gestured theatrically, and then giggled.

"I would like to finish our exploration of the bay," said Tom. "But we should have that down already, because that was our adventure for today, so you can put me down for boating. I would like to get a sail up on *Kitty Kat*, and see how she goes, then we could do a bit of pirating maybe, but any sort of boating will do. A night onboard the *Esperance* would be fantastic! I'm definitely up for that."

Ian was last to speak. He was trying to think of something different to come up with, but he couldn't. "I think that's plenty to be getting on with," he said. "But where would we all sleep, if we spent the night onboard?"

"The girls could sleep in the cabin," said Bart, "And

the rest of us could sleep under the awning. I've done it before, and it's fine if you have a sunbed and a sleeping bag."

"Well, I think the first thing we should do, if it's alright with you, Bart, is to make the *Esperance* our base camp, our headquarters," said Ian. "Then we can all meet up here each day, to start off with."

"It would be a great honour for me, and for the *Esperance*," said Bart, grandly. "What we really need though, is a flag which we can hoist when we are acting as headquarters. We'll have to think of a name for ourselves, and then design a flag to go with it."

They put their heads together and came up with various suitable names.

"The old stone-age expeditionary force!"

"*Esperance* adventurers!"

"Boys and girls together!"

"Sailors and explorers unlimited!"

"How about, explorers of the bay?" said Ian.

Everyone thought about it and nodded. It seemed to cover everything, and sounded quite sensible.

"Right. Explorers of the bay it is," said Anna, getting out her sketchbook. She drew up a design with EB in large letters in a circle, with compass points around it.

"That looks brilliant!" said Tom. "I'll see if my mum can help us make a flag if you like."

Just at that moment Anna's phone sounded. "Hello mother...Yes we're fine... We're on a boat in the middle of the bay... No I'm only joking. It isn't that far out really. It's by the kiosk near the church... OK we'll see you soon then... Bye."

"They're coming to fetch us," she said to Shani. "Sorry boys, we have to go. Can you take us back to the beach please, Bart?"

Bart went to the ladder by the stern of the boat, undid one of the looped ropes tied to it, and hauled in the dinghy, which was a stout little clinker built affair, with a small mast up forrard.

"I'll row us in," he said, "And I'll come back for Ian and Tom afterwards."

The girls climbed onboard as Bart held onto the ladder, and carefully took their places, one at the stern and one at the bow, as directed. Bart sat in the middle, pushed away from Esperance and placed the oars in the rowlocks.

"Cheerio, Tom! Cheerio, Ian!" the girls called out.

"Cheerio, girls! See you tomorrow. Oh hang on a minute. What if you have to go to Herm?"

"We'll phone you. Or I'll phone Bart. What's your number, Bart?" said Anna, and pulled out her sketch book to make a note of it.

It was only a few yards to the beach, but Anna's parents had already arrived in their car, and watched in amazement as the two young ladies alighted from the dinghy, gallantly assisted by a handsome young man, then put on their trainers and walked up the beach.

"What will they get up to next?" said Mrs Riley.

"I think it's amazing," said Mr Riley. "Just look at that old boat sitting in the corner of the bay. What a sheltered spot for a mooring. What a lovely sight."

As they drove back to the hotel, Anna and Shani told them all about their day, and how they had met Bart.

"He looks like a capable sort of boy," said Mr Riley. "I think you've made some jolly good friends on this trip, haven't you, girls?"

Back on the *Esperance*, Tom, Ian and Bart quickly tidied up, and then clambered into the dinghy.

"We'd better get a move on," said Ian. "We have to go and fetch our bikes back at the hotel, and it's quite a long walk."

"Probably quicker if we take the main road," said Tom, somewhat reluctantly, as he didn't relish the thought of getting back to civilisation.

As they rowed in they made plans for the next day.

"Right, we'll be here about ten o'clock, Bart. Then we'll decide what to do, depending on whether the girls can make it or not."

Bart waved goodbye, as Tom and Ian trotted off in the direction of the hotel. The emergency rations of chocolate were consumed on the way.

"There you are, Ian," said Tom. "Always best to have some chocolate handy, for emergencies you know."

Chapter 6

Kitty goes sailing

Tom didn't get home till just after six o'clock. His mother had been expecting him a little earlier and she was just starting to worry, when, luckily, he whizzed into the driveway on his bike, screeched to a halt, and somewhat breathlessly trotted in through the back door. Tom's little sister Becky was helping mum to prepare dinner, while his father sat at the kitchen table reading the paper.

"Sorry I'm a bit late, mum," he panted. "Got held up by the tide. Hello, Becky. Hi, dad. You won't believe where I've been today. On board the *Esperance*. You know. The boat in the corner of the bay. The old Herm boat."

He told them how he and Ian had gone exploring with the girls, and met up with Bart, and how they were going to call themselves Explorers of the Bay, and could he please have an old piece of material to make a flag.

"Well goodness me, you have had an exciting time of it," said mum. "We'll have to see if we've an old sheet or something. Wait a minute, I know the very thing. I've some old curtain linings which I was going to give your dad for dust sheets, but he won't mind, will you, Bill?"

"No that's fine. I've plenty of dust sheets at the moment. If you like, you can use my acrylic paints for the flag, Tom" said Bill Le Page. "By the way, I'm sorry I haven't been able to come up with a sail plan yet. I just don't know what to suggest really. It's not the sail that would be too difficult, it's what to do about the rudders and dagger boards. I can't help thinking you need two of each, one for each hull, and really it's a project for over the winter."

"That's okay, dad. I'm hoping Bart might be able to take us sailing in his dinghy, and maybe Ian and I could just try something for a bit of fun with one of those curtain linings. Even if I have to stand up and hold it myself. Or maybe I could get Ian to be the mast, he's taller and thinner than me! Anyway don't worry about it, we'll be fine."

After dinner Mrs Le Page pulled out the curtain linings. They were each about six feet square, and made of some sort of off-white, coated material, which was perfect for cutting into flag size pieces. This gave Tom another idea. He would cut out a flag for *Kitty Kat*, and paint a skull and crossbones on it. Then he could sail into the bay and capture the *Esperance*. Oh what fun that would be! But he would keep his cunning plan secret for the moment. It would be best to maintain an element of surprise. He felt sure Bart wouldn't mind being captured for a short while, and maybe forced to walk the plank, if it was a nice day.

Tom was quite good at arts and crafts. He enjoyed making things, and as he happily continued with his work, he was mulling over the wonderful possibilities of life as the most feared pirate captain on the west coast, a suitable outfit, the weapons he might need to pursue his new career choice, such as water bombs and perhaps a catapult to fire them off. Soon the flags were cut to size, and he started to paint on the design of EB in a big circle, with compass points, copying from the sketch Anna had provided. Ahaaaarr, he thought to himself. It wouldn't be long before that flag was hauled down, and his own skull and crossbones put in its place.

Becky asked if she could do some painting too, so he cut her a piece of scrap material, and showed her how to put some paint on one side, and then fold it over and press down to make a splodgy mirror image pattern.

"Look, mummy!" said Becky. "It looks like a pansy."

Becky was taken off to bed, and Tom finished off the other side of the explorers' flag. Luckily the paint dried ever so quickly, so there was less risk of smudges. Then he painted his own pirate flag, and left them both carefully draped over the clothes horse, to finish drying completely.

It always takes longer than you think it will, to make things like flags, and before he knew it, it was time for bed. Up in his bedroom, Tom pulled out a book from his bookshelf, about early sailing vessels. He turned to the picture of the Viking longship, which had been so much in his mind of late, and carefully noted how the sail was fixed to the mast and other details of the rigging. It shouldn't be too difficult he thought, as he settled down to sleep.

The next morning, at breakfast, Tom asked his father if it might be possible for him, on his travels, to drop off a couple of pieces of timber down at Rousse.

"Ah, this is for the mast and that, is it?" said Bill Le Page. "Yes. I can drop them off this morning as a matter of fact, but I want you to promise me that you won't set sail without me having a look first, Tom. Now is there anything else you might need? I'll drop off a coil of thin rope for the rigging, and some tools and other bits and pieces which might come in useful. I'll put them in a cardboard box and shove them under the tarpaulin."

"Oh thanks, dad!" said Tom, overjoyed that he was actually going to be allowed to have a go by himself. "I promise we won't try sailing her by ourselves. We'll let you inspect everything first."

At half past nine Ian arrived on his bike.

"Hey Tom, I've asked my mum if it's okay to camp out overnight on the *Esperance*, and she says that's fine as long as we're all onboard together, and Anna's there with her mobile phone in case we have any problems. Have you asked yet?"

Tom explained that after his mum and dad helping with the flags, and letting him put up a sail on *Kitty Kat*, he hadn't really wanted to ask for too much at once.

"Oh come on, Tom, I'll mention it to your mum. If she knows my parents are okay with it, she's bound to say yes."

So Ian explained how they were all going to camp out together, and Anna would have her phone for emergencies, and Tom's mother said she was sure that would be fine, just for one night.

Tom carefully rolled up the Explorers of the Bay flag inside one of the curtain linings, and tied them to the top of his rucksack. The two lads set off with their bikes to meet Bart, and arrived to find him on the beach. It was a beautiful summer's day, with the sun sparkling on the blue waters of the bay, and just a gentle cooling breeze from the north-west.

"The girls have been in touch," said Bart. "They're off to Herm for the day, so that just leaves the three of us. Any ideas? I'd like to do a bit of sailing when the tide comes up. The dinghy's high and dry at the moment."

"Would you like to come and help us with our boat?" asked Tom. "We want to try and fix up a sail. I've worked out how to do it."

"Yeah, that sounds interesting," said Bart.

"What about the flag, Tom?" said Ian. "Show Bart the flag."

Tom untied the curtain lining, and unrolled it to reveal his handywork.

"Wow! That's great, Tom," said Bart. "Let's take it onboard and fly it from the mast. First though we need to sew a piece of rope on, so we can tie it to the flag halyard. I have a needle and thread in the cabin. You never know when you might need them for sail mending and such."

After ten minutes or so, Bart had the flag ready, and they fixed it to the halyard and raised it to the top of the mast. The breeze was just perfect to show it off. All as pleased as punch, they climbed down the ladder and walked to the top of the beach, where they turned around for a better view.

"Now she looks like a real explorers' ship," said Bart.

They made off in the direction of Rousse. They had to share the two bikes between the three of them, taking turns at riding and walking, but they made good progress, and reached their destination just as Tom's father arrived to unload the bits and pieces.

"Hello, Bart. Nice to meet you," said Mr Le Page. "I think I knew your father back in the old days. How is he? I haven't seen him for ages."

"Very well thank you," said Bart. "He lives in France now. I'm going to see him next week."

"Remember me to him, won't you? Tell him Bill Le Page sends his regards. Well lads, that's the lot. I thought those brackets might be handy for fixing the base of the mast to the front seat there, and you can use the brace and bit to drill holes for the rigging, but make sure you drill from both sides to make a neat job of it, and those old galvanised blocks might be handy for the running ropes, and there's some glasspaper for taking the edge off the spars."

"That's brilliant, dad. Thanks ever so much," said Tom.

"Okay lads. Must fly. See you later."

The boys removed the cover. "Blimey," said Bart. "I've never seen anything like this before. I think she's going to fly along. She's so sleek!"

Tom explained what he was aiming to achieve. They needed two sets of holes through the top of the mast for the standing rigging, and a block at the top with a rope through it to hoist up the sail.

"Yes, I see what you mean," said Bart. "Shall I fix the brackets to the front seat, ready for the mast to slot into place?"

"Right, if you do that, Ian and I will drill the holes and start threading the rope through for the stays."

They had to put the mast up, and take it down a few times, before they could cut the ropes to the right length, but before too long, the mast, which was about nine feet high, was up and ready. It seemed nice and steady too, as Tom's dad had left a couple of old bottle screws which they used for final tightening of the backstays.

"Now for the sail," said Tom. "We can fix it to the spar with some string through the holes where you put the curtain hooks, but first we need to drill a hole. No, wait a minute, we can use that galvanised eye to thread the lifting rope through."

It was all so exciting for the boys. They couldn't wait to see the sail hoisted up the mast, so they fairly whizzed along with their work. Tom made a tail at each of the lower corners of the sail, and tied the mainsheet ropes to each tail.

"Right, let's get her up. Hoist the mainsail!" he cried.

The sail went half way up the mast, but then lurched off to one side. They had to lower it again.

"I think we need a loop around the mast, so it stays in position," said Ian.

"Good thinking," said Tom. They cut a short piece of rope and tied it loosely around the mast and onto the yard.

"It might stick a bit, but you can always give it a yank," said Bart.

Finally they hoisted the sail to the top and set the sail in a good shape by adjusting the mainsheets.

"He hey!" crowed Tom. "She looks like a Spanish galleon. Look she's starting to pull at the trailer! I think she's going to work out fine."

"Yes, I don't think she'll need any more canvas than that," said Bart. "Not to start off with anyway. But what are you going to use for a rudder?"

"What about one of the oars?" suggested Ian. "We could drill a couple of holes near the top of the transom, and tie down one of the oars. That way we won't lose it overboard if we have to let go of it."

"Great idea Ian," said Tom. "You sort that out while Bart and I get the mainsail down, otherwise I think she might sail off on the trailer."

After tidying up, they settled down for some lunch. They had all brought sandwiches and drinks and were just finishing off when Tom's father turned up.

"Wow, Tom. She looks really good. I wasn't expecting you to sort her out so quickly. Well done all of you. Look if you want to give her a try, I'll stick around for half an hour, as I haven't had my lunch yet."

Tom, as usual, was rearing to go. "Can we, dad?" he asked, incredulously.

"I don't see why not. As long as you have your lifejackets on. It's a perfect day for it."

After a few final adjustments the three boys wheeled

Kitty down to the water's edge, and went through the launching procedure as Bill Le Page watched them from the pier.

They decided Tom and Bart should try her out first. Bart was the most experienced sailor, so he took the helm, and showed Tom the ropes. They cast off and headed out across the bay on a broad reach. This was about the most they expected from a square rigger, but certainly on that course the little boat performed perfectly adequately, making about two to three knots and hardly heeling over at all. They had gone quite a way out and then turned into the wind. It looked as if there was some slight confusion onboard as the sail flapped and dipped, and even pushed her backwards for a minute, until Tom managed to paddle her around, so she was facing back towards the pier. Then the sail filled again and she sailed sedately back again.

"No problems to speak of, sir," Bart reported. "Not in this light breeze anyway. But she won't point up into the wind, and she needs some persuading to go about."

Bill Le Page was reassured. He could see that Bart knew his stuff.

"Well, Bart, if you would be kind enough to give the lads some lessons before we actually let them loose by themselves, I can see they will be safe enough. I'm going to leave you all to it as I have to get back to work. Now do be careful. Mind how you go."

Bill went back to his van, and sat for a while longer, to eat his lunch and watch the sailing lessons, then, as everything seemed to be under control, he drove off thinking: better leave them to it, you can't be watching over them every minute.

Tom had been ever so excited to be sailing his own boat for the very first time.

"This is what I call boating!" he cried. "What do you think of her, Bart?"

There had only been one moment when he was not too sure of himself. When Bart had tried to tack, there had been so many ropes to let go, and pull in, and tie off, and then Bart had said "Quick Tom! Grab that paddle and paddle like mad!" He was starting to think that sailing was not as simple and straightforward as it might be. But then, as the sail filled again and *Kitty* set off on her new course, bobbing over the little wavelets, with the water bubbling around her bows, and peace descended once again, he thought it was the best thing in the world. This was what he had been dreaming of, and now it was the real thing. He was quite overwhelmed.

"She doesn't seem to be too bad," said Bart. "I would have expected her to make more lee-way, seeing as she doesn't have any keel as such. I reckon her hulls are so narrow, they kind of act like keels in a way. They sort of dig in, and stop her from drifting sideways too much."

Tom nodded and smiled. He didn't quite understand what Bart was talking about, but he was ever so proud of his boat.

When they arrived back at the pier, they had to drop the sail, as this seemed to be the only way to stop her. Tom's father had seemed quite satisfied that all was safe. Then Ian had his turn, while Tom sat on the pier and watched. This time, as soon as they had cleared the rocks, Bart headed into the bay. The sail was straightened up, and with the wind abaft the beam, *Kitty* picked up her skirts and charged off as fast as she would go, but Bart did not take her too far in. He knew that, otherwise, they would have to row back against the wind, so after a short burst, the sails were adjusted again, and he headed back as close into the wind as she would go. Tom could see that Bart was testing *Kitty* to see what could be expected of her, and with each manoeuvre and each trimming of the sails, he and Ian would be gaining experience for when they eventually were allowed to use her by themselves.

It would have been better if they could both learn together, but they only had the two lifejackets with them, and his father had made it pretty clear that there was to be no sailing without lifejackets. Nevertheless, Tom had a good view from the pier, and if he watched carefully, he was sure he could still learn quite a lot from that.

They had been so busy getting the boat ready and then trying her out that he had hardly thought about Anna and Shani. He wondered how they were getting on with their trip to Herm. It was such a beautiful island, and normally Tom would have been quite envious, but his day had been so fantastic that he almost felt sorry for them.

Bart and Ian finally returned to the pier. "What do you think of her, Ian?"

"That was quite something, Tom. Quite something," said Ian, in a bit of a daze.

"Right ho Tom. Your turn," said Bart. "We've given the ropes names. I'm not sure if they are the right names, as I've never sailed a square rigger before, but the ropes on this side I'm calling starboard fore sheet, and starboard back sheet, and the ones on that side, port fore sheet, and port back sheet. So when we go about I'll say: let go the port back sheet, haul in the starboard back sheet and trim the fore sheets."

"I don't understand why we have to have so many sheets," said Tom.

"No. It's not ideal is it," said Bart. "There must be a better way, but at the moment the foresheets help to pull the sail down flat. We'll have to give it some thought."

They spent a further hour or so training and experimenting, and then Bart came up with an idea. "Look, it's just about high tide now. Why don't I sail her back to headquarters, and then you two can cycle around. It'll save me walking, and you won't have to trailer her out. We can run her up the beach and she'll be fine until tomorrow."

"Great," said Ian.

"Fine by me," said Tom. "Then we can meet up at HQ tomorrow, and *Kitty* will be there all ready to go. Okay we'll just watch you go, then we'll cycle round and meet you on the beach."

Everything went according to plan. Bart had a really good run downwind all the way to the beach, and Tom and Ian secured the trailer, and cycled round to meet him. He had already arrived when they got there, anchored the boat, and was rolling up the sail and generally tidying up.

"How about a cup of tea?" said Ian. "I'm parched, and I could do with something to eat too."

"So could I," said Tom. He had felt there was something missing, and now he knew what it was. "I'm absolutely famished," he said, rubbing his tummy. "I've still got some pocket money left. Let's have some Guernsey gache from the trading station."

Chapter 7

Herm Island

As soon as they woke up, Anna and Shani knew that they would not be able to join the rest of the explorers that day. The weather was just about perfect for a trip to Herm. They knew that Anna's parents had been looking forward to it, and there was no way they would be left behind. It wasn't all bad though. Much as they had enjoyed every minute with the boys, and they couldn't wait to get back together, Anna had told Shani how beautiful Herm Island was, and it really didn't seem too much of a hardship to have the chance to explore another island, even if they would have to keep Anna's parents company. And even the parents weren't so bad really.

The ferry was loaded with passengers. So much so they worried that the island might be quite crowded when they got there. They trickled out slowly between the pier-heads of St Peter Port harbour and then the ferry picked up speed. It was a catamaran, very much like a huge version of *Kitty Kat*, with a vast cabin and stairs up to a viewing deck above. Shani and Anna headed straight for the upper deck, while the parents found themselves a nice window seat below. In the open air it was quite breezy as the boat sped along. The girls had to hold onto their sun hats, as they looked back at the foaming wake stretching out behind the boat, and the pretty view of the town of St Peter Port with its hundreds of little quaint old fashioned buildings stretching up from the shoreline.

"Just think, Shani," said Anna. "The *Esperance* would have made this same trip, time and time again, loaded up with people on their holidays, just like us. Isn't that a funny thought? Up and down she would have gone, day after day, week after week."

"Yes, that is a funny thought," said Shani. "You do think of some funny things, Anna!"

"Yes, but don't you think she might be missing the company, you know, all those jolly people laughing and enjoying themselves? Don't you think she might be lonely, tied up, all by herself in that quiet spot?"

"The *Esperance* is a boat, Anna!" laughed Shani. "Boats don't get lonely. In any case she's quite an old boat, and she should be retired now and having a nice rest."

Looking forward they could see Herm and Jethou ahead of them. They decided that Herm, in a way, was like a tiny version of Guernsey. The rocky cliffs of the south coast rose almost vertically out of the sea, and from this high point the land sloped gently down towards a flat grassy area at its northern end. At the centre of the island there was a tiny harbour and a group of buildings, and stretching out all the way to its northernmost point a ribbon of white sand, contrasting sharply against the blue sea. To the right of Herm they could see Jethou, which was like a huge mound rising up to the same impressive height as the cliffs of Herm, and between the two islands a seawater passage, some three or four hundred yards wide, through which they could see the island of Sark in the distance. Dotted all about them were rocks, or posts marking where rocks lay beneath the surface.

"You'd have to know your way around to be safe in these waters," said Anna. "I bet there have been many, many ships wrecked on these treacherous coasts."

The ferry drove on, leaving one post marked with a "C" to port, and one marked "A" to starboard, then another marked "G" to starboard.

"Look Shani. Look over there. You can see the leading marks for Herm harbour. See those white marks one above the other. You have to keep them lined up to avoid the rocks." But the ferry, leaving another post marked "E" to starboard, changed course and headed for the passage between Herm and Jethou. "We must be landing at Rosiere steps," said Anna, "The tide isn't high enough for the harbour yet."

The journey was over all too soon, but as they stepped off the ferry onto the Island, it felt really exciting to be treading on foreign soil.

"Right, girls," said Mr Riley. "Shall we go right about, around the cliffs to Belvoir Bay, or left about, over the common to Shell Beach? Or we can go over the top if you like. The choice is yours."

"I don't mind which," said Shani, "It's all new to me."

"Let's go left about," said Anna, "Then we can show Shani the little harbour and village, and it's a lovely day for walking over the common to Shell Beach."

"Is that alright with you, my dear?" Mr Riley asked Mrs Riley.

"Yes, that will be wonderful. Perhaps we can stop at the Mermaid, for a coffee," said Mrs Riley. "Now we must all be careful of the sun. Herm is well known as a place where you can burn very easily, without even noticing it. Mind you keep well covered up, girls. Here let me just put some sun cream on your arms. And you, dear," she said, turning to Mr Riley, "You must put some cream on your face and neck."

The sun cream was duly applied, and then they paused a while to admire the view of Jethou and Guernsey, before setting off along a wide gravel path. The other passengers had gone ahead, and it was wonderfully quiet and peaceful. The air was fresh, and sweet with the scent of wild flowers. You could hear only the buzzing of insects, the mewing of gulls, and the sound of the sea lapping against the shore. After the hustle and bustle, and traffic of St Peter Port, this was only a few miles away, but a different world.

They soon reached the harbour, and a small group of buildings which made up the harbour village. There was a signpost pointing inland for Belvoir Bay, and another pointing north along the coast for Shell Beach. There were one or two gift shops, which Mrs Riley felt compelled to explore, and then they reached the Mermaid Inn. On the coastal side of the Inn, Anna showed Shani one of the beacons which made up the leading marks.

"They have lights on them at night," said Anna, "So you can still get in and out safely in the dark."

They sat at a table in the walled garden outside the inn, and Mr and Mrs Riley had coffee, while the girls drank some lemonade.

"Do you know," said Mr Riley, "People come over from Guernsey of an evening, in their boats. They leave them tied up in the harbour, and pop in here for a pint. Now that's living isn't it?"

There were a few too many visitors about for Anna's liking, and she was pleased when they were able to leave, and continue their journey along the coastal path. As Shani had noticed from the ferry, there was one long sandy beach all the way along, except for the odd rocky outcrop. The tide was still fairly low, and beyond the beach the rocks stretched out for several hundred metres in places. Shani thought there were probably dozens of rock pools and other delights just waiting to be found.

They reached the common, which was quite like L'Ancresse Common, but there were different kinds of grasses and prickly plants about, and that strange intoxicating scent in the air. They turned right, following the sign for Shell Beach. The sun was beating down, the sky a deep blue, the common stretched out on the left, an undulating pale green expanse of grass and scrub, worn bare to the sand in places. To the right the land rose higher towards the centre of the island, and they walked past a path leading in that direction. Mr Riley paused for a moment. "By Jove it's hot," he said, taking off his hat and mopping his brow with a hanky. His face was even redder than usual. "I think I may go for a dip, when we get there, to cool off a bit," he said.

"It's like Treasure Island," Shani whispered to Anna. "If I were a pirate this is where I would bury my treasure. In the middle of the common. No one would ever find it."

"You'd have to make a map, with clues on it written in code, and dead men's bones for pointers," Anna whispered back.

Presently they reached Shell Beach, which was a fabulous stretch of golden sand sloping gently towards the sea, and as you looked more closely at the sand, you could see that it was made up of millions and millions of ground up shells. They found a good spot on the softer sand at the top of the beach, laid out their towels and bags, and changed into their swimsuits.

The tide was still out and there were one or two boats left drying out further down the beach. Further out still, more boats had anchored in deeper water. Some were flying French flags, some the red ensign, and the Guernsey boats had their own version of the red ensign, with a yellow Norman cross added. It made a wonderful sight, with people on the beach sunbathing, swimming, building sandcastles, and generally having fun.

"Are you coming in, dear?" Mr Riley asked his wife.

"No thank you, darling," she replied. "I'll stay here for the moment. Now make sure you all come back for some more sun cream after your swim."

The three of them walked down the beach, and dipped

their toes into the water, which was colder than expected, so they splashed around for a while in the shallows, just to get accustomed to it. Mr Riley was the first in, and he entertained them with his impersonation of a whale, and then a walrus, which Shani found particularly amusing.

"It's not too bad once you're in," spluttered Mr Riley. "Most refreshing in fact."

The two girls also tried some swimming. They were more accustomed to swimming pools and fresh water swimming, so they found the salt water much easier to float in. Mr Riley was floating on his back, propelling himself with his arms, just like a rowing boat.

After much fun and laughter, they decided it was probably lunch time. They made their way back to Mrs Riley, who supervised the application of more sun cream, and then they walked over to the beach café.

Lunch was a jolly affair, with crisps, sandwiches and fizzy drinks, and chocolate to finish off. It was so hot they had to lick the melting chocolate off their fingers. The café had a nice seating area outside, with sunshades, and palm trees in pots, and a wonderful view over the bay. It was like a tropical paradise.

After lunch, Mr and Mrs Riley had a snooze, while Anna and Shani went exploring along the beach. They searched for shells as they went along, but the tide was coming up now, and they had missed the best pickings. The further they went, the fewer people were about, until, as they reached the northern end of the beach they were finally alone.

"This is what Robinson Crusoe must have felt like,"

said Shani. “Shipwrecked on a desert island.”

They sat and chatted, and admired the view, then started to make their way back. They noticed quite a few people were packing up and getting ready to leave.

“Just enough time for another swim, I reckon,” said Anna.

“Yes. How about swimming around that fishing boat and back?” said Shani.

She pointed to a little open fishing boat, brightly painted in red, white, and blue, just a short distance from the beach.

“Come on then. Race you!” said Anna.

They put their things in a pile, then ran down the beach into the water, and swam towards the boat. In the shallows the water had been warmed, pulled in by the tide over the hot sand. As they swam further out the water became colder.

After a few minutes, Anna thought to herself that they must be out of practice. They didn’t seem to be moving as quickly as they should. She tried putting more effort into it, and slowly, their distance from the shore increased.

A few minutes later they were still struggling to make headway. Shani had noticed it too but was swimming gamely on.

“What’s going on, Shani? This boat seems further away than I thought. Come on. Let’s try and get a move on.”

They were halfway to the boat before Anna realised what was happening. “Shani!” she called. “I don’t think we’re going to make it. The tide’s pushing us sideways. I think we’d better go back.”

"Come on, Anna," Shani called back, "We can do it."

Anna wasn't too sure about this, but she could see that Shani was still confident, so she redoubled her efforts. A few more minutes passed by, and she started to see that although they were having to swim twice as fast as usual, they were ever so slowly inching towards the boat. The trouble was, that the further out they went, the stronger the current had become.

On and on they swam. Now they couldn't stop for a second, or they would be swept away. Side by side, they matched each other, stroke for stroke. It was no good heading back to the beach now. They were too tired, and the tide would take them off.

"Come on, Shani. Just a bit further," gasped Anna. "Come on. One last push."

"I don't know if I can," Shani spluttered.

Then they heard a shout from the boat.

"Hang on girls! I'm going to throw you a rope. Now you both grab hold of it, and I'll haul you in."

Then they heard a shout from the beach. "Anna! Shani! Are you alright?"

But they were oblivious to the shouting. They had one thought only. The rope was their only chance. It splashed down in front of them. Just a few inches and they would be safe. With all their remaining strength they lunged out and grabbed hold of it.

"Well done, girls! Now hold on tight, and I'll have you onboard in no time at all," called the fisherman. A strong arm reached down, first to Shani, then to Anna, and hoiked them up into the boat, where they stood shaking and shivering, and gasping for breath.

"Well now, this is the prettiest catch I've had for some time," said the fisherman, handing them a huge and colourful beach towel. "Dry yourselves off, and you'll find the sun will soon warm you up. Here put my jacket on, and you, young lady, put on this old Guernsey. Now, is that your mum and dad on the beach?" He waved to Mr and Mrs Riley, just to let them know everything was alright. "Hold on just a moment, Sir, and I'll bring them in."

Suddenly Anna burst into tears. "Oh, I'm so sorry," she sobbed. "I've been so stupid. I knew we should have gone back." Shani, feeling uncomfortable that she was partly to blame, put her arm around Anna, to comfort her, and found her eyes also pricked with tears.

"Oh, come along now," said the fisherman in a kindly fashion. "There's no need to upset yourselves. You're on holiday, aren't you?" The girls nodded. "Well then, you weren't to know the tide can rip through here like that. These are beautiful islands, but the waters can be dangerous. Big tides and fast currents. Enough to catch anyone out. But you're safe now. You just dry your eyes. And we'll say nothing about it to your mum and dad. I think you've learned your lesson, and there's no point in them getting all worried and upset."

But Mr and Mrs Riley were getting worried.

"Hello there!" shouted Mr Riley. "Sorry to trouble you, but if we don't leave now, we'll miss the last ferry back."

"Just got to wait a minute or two!" the fisherman called back, thinking a few minutes would be needed for the girls to compose themselves. "Not enough water for me to come in just yet, but I'll be with you in a jiffy!"

He started to walk about the boat, tidying up and getting things ready, then he checked the fuel gauge and started up the engine. Then he went over to the girls and put a kindly hand on their shoulders.

"Well, girls. Are you feeling a little better?"

They nodded sheepishly, but they were starting to feel better. They had warmed up, and they knew that now they were safe.

"Right. Well I think you'd be better not having to rush for the last ferry, so I'll take her in, and we'll ask your mum and dad if they want a lift back."

Now the girls really did start to perk up. A lift back in a fishing boat! Perhaps things were not so bad after all.

The fisherman left his anchor down, but untied the rope at the bow, and passed it through a fairlead on the stern of his boat. Then he pushed the gear lever forward, and started to chug slowly towards the beach, paying out the anchor rope as he went, to keep the stern pointing out to sea. Soon the boat was touching the sand at the bows, and the fisherman went forward to talk to Mr and Mrs Riley.

"Sorry to make you late, Sir, Ma'am," he said, and went on to convince them that it would be far easier, and less of a rush, if they would like to travel back in his boat.

"Well that is most kind of you," said Mr Riley. "It's entirely my daughter's fault of course, as usual. What were you thinking of, Anna, going off swimming again?"

A ladder was dropped over the bow to help them aboard. Mrs Riley helped the girls to get dressed, and eventually everyone was seated comfortably, and ready to go. Introductions were made. The fisherman, who was called Phil, pulled the boat out on the anchor rope, and then pulled up the anchor. The boat was put into gear, and chugged along following the edge of the bay, then they headed out through a narrow passage, passed Belvoir Bay, and threaded their way around and between the rocks off the east coast of the island. Obviously, Phil was intimately acquainted with these waters. At times they could almost have reached out and touched the cliffs and the rocks, as passed them by, with the steady chug of the engine and the bluff bows of the little fishing boat creaming through the still waters.

"I see your boat is called *Cobo Alice*," said Mrs Riley. "Do you keep her at Cobo Bay?"

"No, ma'am," said Phil. "I used to keep her at Cobo, but at the moment I keeps her in a little bay up by Bordeaux Harbour. It's just a bit more sheltered, and a bit more 'andy for where I live."

They turned into the passage between Herm and Jethou, which, Phil informed them, was called Percee Passage, and then they headed through a narrower passage between Jethou and Crevichon, a tiny island shaped like a cone, with steep sides rising to its peak.

"They call this the neck of Jethou," said Phil. "You can get through any time after half tide up, but look how it races through here. I used to come over for a drink with my dad, when they had a pub on Jethou. We used to sail over, then quite often the wind would drop, and we would have to hope somebody might give us a tow

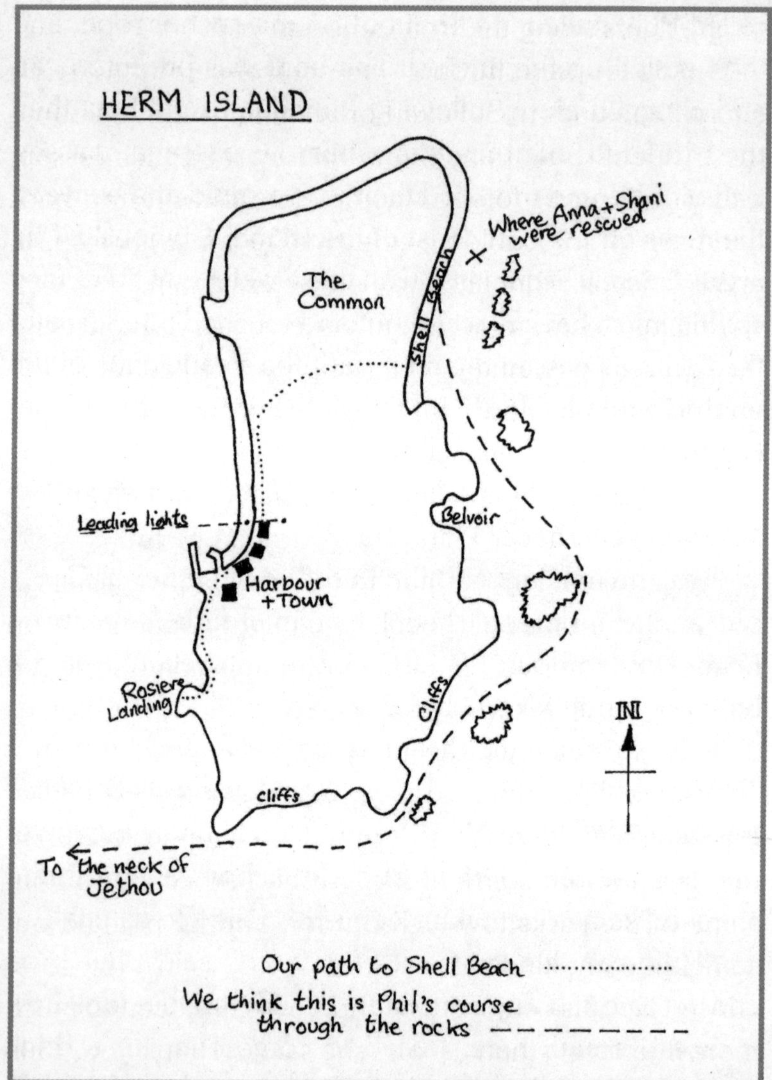
HERM ISLAND
Where Anna + Shani were rescued
The Common
Shell Beach
Leading lights
Belvoir
Harbour + Town
Rosiere Landing
Cliffs
N
cliffs
To the neck of Jethou
Our path to Shell Beach
We think this is Phil's course through the rocks

back. Usually somebody did. Otherwise it was a long row back. It was lovely mind, with the sea like black oil, and all the lights along the front reflected in it."

Once they were through the neck of Jethou, it was a straight run back to St Peter Port. Nothing was said about the incident. Shani and Anna had learned their lesson, and would never forget it completely, but the trip back had been so enjoyable that they had regained their spirit, and felt much more like their old selves again.

Phil told them stories about smugglers and shipwrecks.

"Is there any smuggling these days?" asked Mr Riley.

"Not so much now," said Phil, "But I have heard there is the odd crab pot pulled up which don't have no crabs in it."

"Really?" said Mr Riley. "How do you mean?"

"Well, they might happen to go off to France, shall we say, and when they gets back they might happen to drop off a pot on their way into the harbour, in some secluded little bay, if you know what I mean. Then they comes back later on and whisks it ashore."

"My goodness me," said Mr Riley.

Phil could see his passengers were keen to learn. He told them about some of the fish he had caught, about some of the rocks to watch out for, and he pointed out some different kinds of seabirds.

Mrs Riley also enjoyed the trip. "This has been so much more interesting than usual," she said. "Thank you, Phil. And it was so kind of you to invite the girls onboard in the first place."

"No problem," said Phil. He gave the girls a knowing

wink, and they smiled back. "I've two daughters of my own, and I like girls with a bit of spirit, like yours."

Landing back on Guernsey, they thanked Phil again, and waved him away from the quay. Anna and Shani wondered what the boys had been up to, but it was too late to go down to the *Esperance*, and anyway, they were really quite exhausted.

"You girls are awfully quiet," said Mrs Riley. "I hope you haven't had too much sun. Are you feeling ill at all?"

"No, Mother. We're fine. Just a bit tired," said Anna.

Later on, after dinner at the hotel, Anna phoned Bart to make arrangements for the next day.

"How was your day?" asked Bart.

"Incredible," said Anna. "We've had such an incredible day. Some of it was quite scary, but we had an amazing trip back in a little fishing boat called *Cobo Alice*. We'll tell you all about it tomorrow."

Chapter 8

Exploring the Bay

The next day dawned bright and clear. There was not a breath of wind. Anna and Shani looked out through the window of their hotel bedroom. It was a gorgeous view over the bay. To the left they could see the rocks and the sea, the Atlantic ocean, then closer in Rousse pier and the fishing fleet, and on the other side L'Ancresse Common and Les Amarreurs. In the far corner of the bay, they could see the *Esperance*, still afloat, but not for much longer, as the tide was going out. Then they saw something else on the beach. It was hard to see, but it looked as though another boat had been pulled up alongside their HQ.

"What a cheek!" said Shani. "We can't be explorers if there's somebody sitting there watching us."

"Oh, no. What are we going to do?" said Anna. "We'll have to have a meeting, and see what the others think."

At breakfast Anna, who was feeling much better after a good night's sleep, plucked up courage to raise the matter of sleeping onboard the *Esperance*.

"But, darling. What's the point of us paying for a hotel room, and you wanting to sleep on some old wreck of a boat?"

"She is not a wreck, Mother. She is a Dunkirk little ship, and a very brave old lady. Surely you can see she needs a bit of company now and then."

Anna's mother reflected on this for a moment. She certainly didn't want to upset any old ladies. Her emotions were slightly confused.

"Well I don't know. What do you think, darling?" she asked Mr Riley. Anna's hopes were immediately raised.

"Well..." said Mr Riley, somewhat hesitantly. "I suppose, for one night it wouldn't matter too much. They seem to be a decent bunch of lads, and as long as Anna takes her phone for emergencies."

"Hmm.Well, we'll think about it," said Mrs Riley. "But before I agree to anything, we really need to inspect the boat. I'm not too sure about this. And what about Shani? I may have to phone your parents, Shani. Oh no I forgot, they've gone away. Well anyway, we'll think about it."

Anna was quite satisfied with this. At least the idea hadn't been rejected. She might need to work on mother, but things were looking quite positive.

"Well, mother. If you would like to, maybe Bart can show you over the boat this morning, when you drop us off."

"But, darling. I thought you were coming with us to the Strawberry Farm today."

Anna wrinkled her nose.

"It's not really our sort of thing, mother. You go with

father, and have a nice day out, just the two of you. Shani and I will be fine around here. We've lots more exploring to do, and we want to have a closer look at the historical sites. You know, the stone-age remains, and the German fortifications."

Mrs Riley could not help being impressed by her daughter's burgeoning interest in history, but still she did not feel quite right, being deprived of her company.

"Come along, darling," said Mr Riley. "We had a nice day out with the girls yesterday. You can see we're not required today. It's good for them to develop a little independence."

The sky had clouded over by the time they reached the *Esperance*, but it was still dry and warm, and there was not a breath of wind.

"Look! It was *Kitty Kat* we saw on the beach," said Shani. "I didn't recognise her at first. Look. She has a mast and sails and everything!"

Anna's father walked down to have a look at *Kitty*. "This is an interesting design," he said. "I bet she's fun to sail in, but she looks a bit flimsy for someone of my great weight."

Tom and Ian arrived on their bikes, and told Mr Riley all about *Kitty*, and how they had made the sailing rig with the help of Tom's father. Then Bart arrived, and Anna asked if her parents could have a look over the *Esperance*. Bart could tell this was fairly crucial, by the look on Anna's face, and he could not have been a more charming host.

"Certainly, Mr and Mrs Riley, please come this way. No, it's no trouble at all."

The *Esperance* had dried out by this time, and Mr and Mrs Riley were able to walk down, and climb up the ladder.

"What a lovely old boat," said Mr Riley. Bart hoisted the flag. Mr Riley was impressed. "My goodness me. You boys have been busy," he said.

Mrs Riley was pleased to see the separate sleeping quarters in the cosy cabin, with its two separate berths. It all seemed reasonably clean and tidy, and her mind was set at rest.

After making arrangements with the girls to meet up for dinner at the hotel, Anna's parents finally left them to it.

"Phew, sorry about that," said Anna. "That's nearly half the day gone, but at least they seem happy enough, and I think we'll be allowed at least one night on board. So... what are we going to do now?"

"I vote we explore the rest of this side of the bay, for starters," said Tom.

Seeing as there was no wind for sailing, and it wasn't really hot enough for swimming, the others thought this was a good idea.

This time Tom had brought his sea chart with him, and the compass. Anna had brought her sketchbook, Shani had the map, and they all had packed lunches of one sort or another in their bags and rucksacks. So, suitably equipped for their expedition, they started off along the northern edge of the bay. On the way, Anna and Shani told the boys about their adventures of the previous day, and the boys told them what a great time

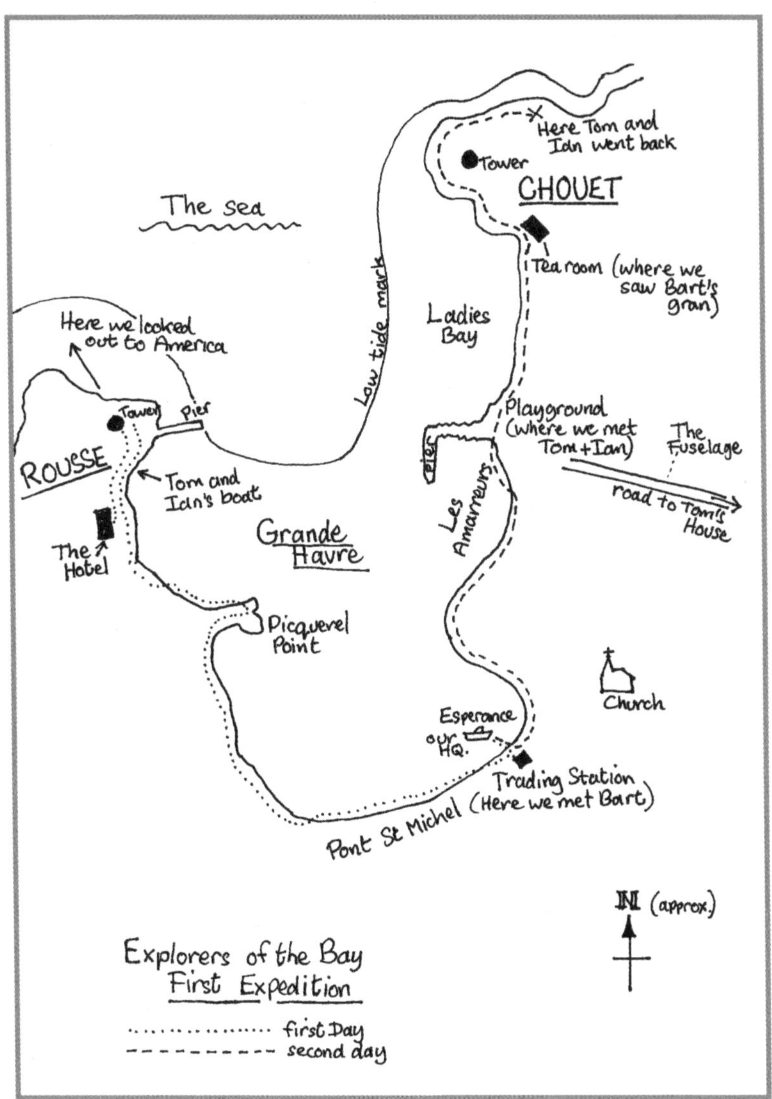

Here Tom and Ian went back
Tower
CHOUET
The sea
Tea room (where we saw Bart's gran)
Low tide mark
Ladies Bay
Here we looked out to America
Tower
Pier
ROUSSE
Tom and Ian's boat
Playground (where we met Tom + Ian)
Pier
The Fuselage
road to Tom's House
Les Amarreurs
Grande Havre
The Hotel
Picquerel Point
Church
Esperance our HQ.
Trading Station (Here we met Bart)
Pont St Michel
N (approx.)
Explorers of the Bay
First Expedition
first Day
second day

they'd had, sailing in *Kitty*.

There were some pretty little cottages to admire along the path, and presently they reached Les Amarreurs, and went down for a closer look. This was one of Tom's favourite beaches, with lovely soft sand sloping gently down to the water's edge. The ancient pier, running from west to east, was a ramshackle structure, built of massive roughly hewn stones. From its western point back to the beach, a line of rocks and boulders, and a shingle bank provided further protection from the sea. The whole arrangement provided a quaint little harbour for about a dozen fishing boats, safe from all but the worst of the winter gales.

Anna sat down to make a few sketches, then she filled in the dotted line on her map to mark their progress, while the boys had a closer look at some of the boats which had dried out.

"Tide's coming up now," said Bart. "These'll soon be afloat."

Shani looked at the map. "The next bay is called Ladies Bay," she said. "I wonder why that is."

"It's very shallow," said Ian. "You can walk out for miles, and the water's still only up to your knees. Well, not miles exactly, but you know what I mean."

"No strong tides then? To sweep the ladies away?" said Shani, thinking of Shell Beach.

"I suppose being shallow and with no strong currents, that would make it especially safe for ladies," Tom suggested.

"Or maybe in the olden days, it was only ladies who

were allowed to bathe there," said Shani. "Like when they had separate bathing for men and ladies."

"Hmmm. Maybe," said Anna. But she wasn't really interested. Her thoughts had turned to the ancient stones that made up the harbour of Les Amarreurs. "I wonder when those boulders were put there to make a breakwater. And how were they moved there? Look, they are all in a straight line. Could be this place is a lot older than people think."

Anna finished her sketching, and they picked up their bags and continued on their way. They walked along Ladies Bay, and marvelled at how quickly the tide was racing up over the flat sand.

"That's another thing you have to be careful of," said Ian to Anna and Shani. "You could be out on those rocks over there, and suddenly find the tide has come in behind you, and you're stuck. Quite often they have to get the inshore lifeboat to rescue people from the rocks."

They reached the end of the beach and walked up the slipway, past another trading station, and then came upon a tearoom overlooking the bay. It was full of elderly ladies having lunch.

"Look out!" said Anna. "It might be the elders of a tribe of cannibals."

"No it isn't," said Bart. "It's the W.I. and that's my gran. Oh no, she's seen us."

It wasn't that Bart didn't like his grandmother. Of course he loved her, but when you're in the middle of an expedition, the last person you want to meet is your gran.

"Oh no. She's waving at us. I'd better go and say hello.

Hang on. Just wait here for me."

Bart trotted dutifully off into the tearoom, where his grandmother took great delight in showing him off to her friends. It wasn't often she had the chance to do this, what with Bart living in England now, and she was immensely proud of her handsome grandson.

"So those are your new friends, Bart? Well isn't it nice that you have someone to play with. Now you must bring them home for tea, before you leave."

After what seemed an eternity, Bart finally managed to wriggle free and escape from the cannibals, and to rejoin the party of explorers, who all waved cheerily at the elderly ladies, before setting off again.

They came upon a notice board, advising them that they were now entering a pistol shooting range, and that the land belonged to the National Trust.

"It's okay," said Bart. "We only have to keep out if the flags are flying, and I don't see any."

"I see no ships!" said Tom, larking about, pretending to be Lord Nelson, and putting an imaginary telescope to his blind eye. Shani giggled. She thought Tom was great fun.

"No, honestly, we can carry on," said Bart. "I've been here before. There's a path that goes all the way round."

The National Trust land was quite nice and wild, and suitable for explorers. They passed another Martello Tower.

"This is Tower No.10, according to the map," said Shani. "I wonder how many there are altogether."

"I think there used to be about fifteen. But some of

them are missing," said Ian.

"Yes. I know where the first one was," said Tom, "Because there's a lane near Belle Greve Bay, called First Tower Lane."

"I like Martello Towers," said Anna. "They are all made of that lovely mellow coloured stone, and you can imagine the soldiers, marching around in their bright red tunics and white trousers, and black hats, and black shiny boots, with their swords and their muskets. All those years ago! In this very spot!" Her eyes shone with the wonderment of it all.

Tom had found a good sized stick by the side of the path, which he had been using to knock the seed heads off the wild flowers and weeds along the way. He ordered himself to "Slope Arms!" put the stick on his shoulder to be his musket, and marched off, making trumpet noises. Ian marched off with him, and Shani skipped after them, laughing, with Bart and Anna following behind.

They rounded the corner of the headland, and came upon a massive bunker overlooking the point, all locked up and fenced off. It was in much better condition than others they had seen, and looked pretty much as they imagined it would have looked during the war. Alongside was a quarry where the pistol shooting took place. Above and below were more German fortifications.

"This must have been an important place to the Germans," said Ian, "To build all of these bunkers. I reckon the headland's probably full of tunnels and stuff. They must have had some pretty big guns here."

"You can see for miles in all directions," said Bart. "It's

the perfect place for a gun battery."

"A perfect spot for lunch," said Tom. "Come on, everyone. It's hungry work, all this exploring."

They unpacked their sandwiches, drinks, fruit and chocolate, and settled down on a grassy bank, to enjoy the food and the view. Tom noticed the rising tide, and this made him think of his plans for turning pirate and raiding the *Esperance*. Obviously she would have to be afloat, or it wouldn't be a proper sea battle. The high tides in the afternoon were getting later each day, and the opportunity for action at sea would be gone in a few days' time, as the *Esperance* would be high and dry for most of the day.

He really needed some time, first of all, to prepare his ship. Ian had agreed to help him, and perhaps now was the time to mention it to the others. They had to know something was going to happen, but not the whole story, because then it wouldn't be so much fun.

Then it occurred to him what to do. He remembered reading about Long John Silver, and how he had sent a special letter, called the Black Spot, but he couldn't remember the words. He thought what he could write, to make it sound like the sort of letter you might expect to receive from a pirate. Hmmm... yes that should do it.

"What shall we do now?" said Bart. "I wouldn't mind carrying on around the point, and taking the road back. Or maybe we could cut across the common."

"Well I've been thinking," said Tom. "Ian and I need to take *Kitty* back to Rousse, and sort out a few things."

"Aren't you coming with us?" asked Shani,

disappointed.

"No, we can't," said Ian, guessing what was on Tom's mind. "But we'll see you tomorrow."

"Yes, we'll leave you a note on the *Esperance*, to let you know what time," said Tom, smiling. "We've finished exploring the bay anyway. That was all we had planned for today. So, see you tomorrow then."

Ian and Tom gathered their things together, dusted themselves off, said their goodbyes, and left.

"I didn't say anything to upset them did I?" asked Anna, as Ian and Tom disappeared around the corner.

"Not that I can think of," said Shani.

"Hmm. They seem to be acting a bit strange," said Bart. "I caught them muttering to each other earlier on, and then they clammed up. I'm not sure what it is, but I think they're up to something."

"Well, if they want to be like that, we'll just do some exploring by ourselves," said Shani. "And I hope we find something really exciting too, while they're not here, and then we can tell them all about it, and how they missed out."

As soon as they were out of sight, Tom quickly explained his plan to Ian.

"We've got to get back to my place quickly, Ian. Then we must write the Black Spot, and pin it on the *Esperance* before the others get back, then we have to get *Kitty* sorted. Quick, there's no time to lose."

They broke into a trot, and were soon back at the *Esperance*, where they collected their bikes, and pedalled like mad to Tom's house.

The Black Spot was written, and a nice black spot put on the front of it with a piece of charcoal borrowed from Bill Le Page's paint box. They grabbed some drawing pins, some string, the pirate flag, and some other bits and pieces for *Kitty*. Then it was back to the *Esperance*, which by now was well afloat.

"Right," said Tom. "We'll use *Kitty* to get out there and leave our note."

"What about our bikes?" panted Ian.

"We'll hide them over there in the bushes, and sneak back later for them," Tom replied.

Everything went according to plan. Luckily the others hadn't got back yet, so Tom and Ian were able to pin the Black Spot to the boarding ladder. "Hope they'll see it alright from the beach," said Tom. Then they paddled off towards Rousse.

Chapter 9

Some Unexpected Discoveries

In fact, Bart and the girls were miles away. They had continued along the coastal path, and were enjoying themselves so much that they carried on towards Pembroke Bay.

"This is great," said Bart. "I'm planning to sail around the north coast some time, and this gives me a chance to see where the rocks are. I was hoping to sail fairly close in with my dinghy, but look at that reef over there. I'd have to feel my way very carefully through that."

Anna was thinking about the dolmens. "Did you find that book on the dolmens, Bart?" she asked.

"Oh yes, sorry. I forgot to bring it with me. I haven't actually had a look at it yet," said Bart.

They made it around the headland, and could see Pembroke Bay, stretching out before them. They reached another Martello tower.

"This is Tower No. 9, according to the map," said Shani. "We must be going backwards, because the last one was No.10."

Opposite the tower was a smaller sandy beach, separated from the main bay by a long finger of land, pointing out to sea.

"There's some sort of building right at the end," said Shani. "It looks like an old fort. Hang on a minute. I'll look on the map and see what it's called." The others gathered around the map. "Yes. It says Fort Pembroke (disused), and there's something else, on the way there, some marks and writing, but it's so faint I can't make it out."

"Let's go and check it out. I've never actually been out there," said Bart. "It's silly really, but there's lots of the island I haven't seen."

Anna was always happy to explore, so they carried on out towards the fort. On the way they looked to see what the other marks on the map might have indicated. There was nothing much to see, except a large circular hollow and various other mounds and dips around and about.

"I think this might also have been a fort at some time," said Anna. "This hollow in the centre might have been a building with walls around it, and these other bits could have been walls and trenches. This would be a perfect place for an archaeological dig."

"The only ones digging at the moment are the rabbits. Look at all of these rabbit holes," said Shani. "And look over there!" Her voice turned to a whisper. "It's a rabbit!"

They all looked at the rabbit, which froze in its tracks for a moment, then scurried off and dived into one of the rabbit holes.

"Oh. I hope it's alright," said Anna. "They're only

supposed to come out at night, aren't they?"

"No," said Bart. "They'll sneak outside for a feed anytime they can. I shouldn't worry too much. There must be thousands of them on the common."

They walked out to the point and reached Fort Pembroke.

"Oh no. It's all locked up," said Shani.

This was a disappointment. They had been looking forward to exploring the fort. All they could see was a high wall with broken glass on the top, and a stout door with iron bars on it. They couldn't even walk around the fort, as the sides dropped straight down into the sea. There was no way around.

"Never mind," said Anna. "Let's go back and have a closer look at those other bits where we saw the rabbit."

So they made their way back, walking around the other side this time where the path dipped down so that the old ruins, or whatever they were, formed a steep grassy bank to one side. Then they came to a passage way almost closed off with brambles but with just a narrow path leading through.

"This looks interesting," said Anna.

She led the way through, which took them to a ramshackle group of old granite buildings, nestling in amongst the grassy banks and mostly covered with brambles and scrub, so they would be virtually invisible to anyone passing by.

"Wow, this is great," chuckled Anna. "What a find! I wonder if we can get inside."

"I don't think so, Anna," said Shani, pointing to a large

'Private' sign, roughly painted and nailed to the door.

"Oh no!" said Anna. "Not again! We're not having much luck today, are we?"

Hang on. Look, the door's open," said Bart. Sure enough, on closer examination they could see that the door had been left slightly ajar. Bart couldn't resist just taking a peep inside. He was about to do so, but suddenly stopped, as he heard the sound of a man's voice coming from inside. It was a rough growly voice and it sounded as if he was talking on the phone.

"Alright mate. Yeah, just leave it to us. Yeah, everything's cool. We'll do the job on Monday. Yeah, get back by then I reckon."

Feeling slightly awkward, Bart turned round and gestured to the others that there was somebody inside. "I think we'd better go," he whispered as loudly as he dared.

Anna and Shani were standing a few yards away and they could not quite understand what was going on.

"What's up, Bart?" said Shani in a loud clear voice, coming closer to try and hear what Bart was saying.

"There's somebody in there!" hissed Bart.

Finally they understood that Bart was trying to get them to leave.

They turned to go, but had only gone a few paces when a very loud and angry voice shouted at them: "'Ere! You lot! What do you think you're up to!"

They spun around to see a rough looking man in overalls had appeared at the door.

"Can't you read!" he bellowed at them, pointing at the sign. "It says PRIVATE. That means you ****** well keep out of 'ere! ****** little nosey parkers!"

"But-" said Bart.

"Don't you give me none of your lip!" shouted the man.

"But, we only wanted to have a look. That's all," said Bart.

"Don't give me that. I know what you're up to, with your broken bottles and your mess you leave behind, and your aerosol spray paints. ****** little vandals, that's what you are!"

"Look, I'm sorry if you've had trouble from other children, but we don't even live here," said Bart.

The man looked slightly puzzled for a moment. He frowned, turned to one side and spat on the ground.

"Oh yeah," he said contemptuously. "Expect me to believe that?"

"Yes it's true," said Anna. "We're on holiday. None of us lives here, so we can't have done anything to upset you."

"Hmm," said the man, thinking things over. Then he leered at them. "Well that ain't the point. This is private property so you can just clear off."

Anna didn't like the look of this man, and she didn't like his disgusting manners. "I think we'd better be getting back," she said.

She turned around and walked off in a very determined manner, taking the others with her. They hardly spoke as they walked back. They were so shocked at this very unpleasant incident.

When they were at a safe distance, Anna stopped and

turned to make sure they were not being followed.

"Quick. Get down!" she said. "He's coming after us."

They dived for cover into the hollow they had found earlier, and peered carefully over the top to see what was happening. The man had come out, carrying some sort of metal box. He put the box down while he lit up a cigarette, then picked it up again and made his way towards them.

"Oh no," said Anna. "Looks like we might have to run for it."

Luckily, the man turned, took another path, and then seemed to disappear behind some gorse bushes.

"Thank goodness for that," said Shani. "What a horrible man!"

"You know what he can do with his tatty old ruins?" said Anna.

"I don't think they even were his," said Shani. "I don't think he had any more right to be there than us. Probably, he was just working there, or something like that."

"Did you see what he was wearing under his overalls?" said Bart. "It looked like a wetsuit."

"Really?" said Anna. "That's very strange. Perhaps we'd better follow him and see what he's up to. There's something odd about this."

They rose to a crouching position, peered around to make sure all was clear, and keeping as low as possible they made their way silently towards the path which the man had taken. Just as they reached the spot, they were startled by the sound of a powerful engine spluttering into life. The noise appeared to come from the beach which was hidden on the other side of a grassy bank before them. They dropped down, crawled up the bank, and peered over the edge. There they saw the man from the ruins, at least they thought it must be him, as the path he had taken led directly onto the beach, and there he was onboard a black inflatable craft which was moored in the shallows with its engine running. They watched as he pulled the craft out to deeper water, lifted out the anchor and took the controls. The engine roared. The boat turned in a tight circle and sped out of the bay.

"Did you see that? Weird or what?" said Bart.

"What do you think he's up to?" said Shani.

"I've no idea," said Bart. "I could hear him talking on his phone to someone about a job or something, but what sort of work you would do in an old ruined fort or in a boat like that I wouldn't know. He wasn't very nice, was he?" said Bart.

"That's putting it mildly," said Anna. "There's something not quite right about this. I don't know why, but something just doesn't feel right. I wonder why he was so bothered about us seeing inside the place? It was almost like he was hiding something. I wonder what he had in that box?"

"Nothing much I don't think," said Shani. "The way he was carrying it, I would say it was empty."

They reached Martello Tower No. 9 again, and consulted the map before deciding which way to go back.

"Let's just head straight back over the common," said Bart. "If we head for the standing stone on the top of that hill, then we'll be able to see our way straight back to HQ."

"Wait a moment," said Shani. "Look at the map here. It shows the standing stone, right, which it calls the Millennium Stone. Then next to it there's a red blob with a number on it, see, just there, and next to it there's some faint writing."

"Oh wow!" exclaimed Anna. "It says La Varde, Passage Grave. Do you think that's another dolmen, Bart?"

"Could be," said Bart. "I think there is one called La Varde."

"Well what are we waiting for?" said Anna. "Let's get going!"

They climbed up the hill towards the Millennium Stone, as quickly as they could, crossed over one of the fairways of the golf course, looking both ways to make sure there was no danger of flying golf balls, and came finally to the summit. There was the standing stone, with '2000' inscribed on it. It was a fair size, but, inspecting the base, they could see it had been bedded in concrete.

"Don't think much of that," said Anna. "Look at that crack in it. I can't see this lasting thousands of years."

There was a fine view over the common from up there, and they noticed some more German fortifications nearby, but no sign of a dolmen.

"It must be here somewhere," said Bart. "Let's circle around the stone, and as we go further and further out, we're bound to find it."

They tried this for a few minutes, and came to a rocky outcrop, which was overgrown with brambles. Shani walked around and below it. "This is it!" she cried.

They raced around, to find her standing at what looked like the entrance to a cave, which went into the hill. They had to bend down slightly to enter the dolmen. It was dark, but as they made their way further in, they could stand upright, and their eyes became accustomed to the darkness. Now, they could see that it wasn't a cave at all. It had been built out of huge stones, all of the walls and the roof. The stones forming the roof were particularly massive.

"How on earth did they do it?" said Bart. "Moving stones like this would be difficult enough today. How did they do it in stone-age times?"

"Look at this," said Shani. "This prop is holding up the roof. Look, where the stone is cracked."

They examined the prop, which was made of granite but looked much newer than the rest.

"It has a date on it," said Anna. "1898."

"It's quite a big dolmen isn't it," said Shani. "It must be about 10 metres long. There's a funny musty smell in here, though. I think I've seen enough."

Bart and Shani made their way out, leaving Anna to ponder. With reverence, she touched the ancient stones and dreamt of the past. She tried to imagine the early humans who had stood on this spot, thousands of years before, and wondered what their lives had been like.

"Come on, Anna!" called Shani eventually. "We'd better be getting back. It's quite a long walk you know."

Anna reluctantly appeared from out of the dolmen.

"That was fantastic," she said. "What a fantastic find. Wait till we tell Tom and Ian!"

They headed back across the common, being careful to avoid the fairways as much as possible, then they came upon the race course, and followed that back to Les Amarreurs. They looked across at Rousse but could see no sign of *Kitty Kat* or the others.

As they were on the final leg back to the *Esperance*, Anna's mobile rang.

"Hello, Mother. Yes we're having a lovely time, thanks. Oh is it? My goodness, I didn't realise how late it was. Okay then. If you can give us half an hour and meet us by the *Esperance* then. Okay. Bye for now. Bye."

"Right," she told the others. "They're coming to collect us in half an hour."

"We'd better hurry up," said Shani. "We have to go

and see if Tom's left us a note, like he said he would."

By the time they arrived back at HQ they were tired out. It had been a long hike, and the girls were pleased that Anna's parents would be giving them a lift back to the hotel. The *Esperance* was afloat in her cosy corner of the bay, and a very pretty sight she made, reflected in the still waters. They looked around on the beach for a note, and then remembered that Tom had said he would leave it on the boat.

"That means I'll have to row out and get it," said Bart.

"I can see it," said Shani. "Look, there's something attached to the boarding ladder."

"Well at least I won't have to climb the ladder," said Bart, hauling the dinghy in to the shore, and hopping in.

Bart pulled himself out to the *Esperance* using the rope tied to the boarding ladder, undid the note and looked at it. This was a funny sort of a note, folded over and stuck down with sticky tape, and on the front of it a big smudgy black blob. He stuffed it in his pocket, and pulled himself back on the rope made fast on the shore.

"Well" said Shani, "What does it say?"

"I haven't opened it yet," said Bart. "It's stuck down with tape."

"Pass it here," said Anna. "I'll open it." Bart handed the note to Anna, and climbed out of the dinghy.

On the front of the note, above the black spot, it said "To the crew of the *Esperance*."

"I know what this is," said Anna, as she carefully pulled back the tape so as not to damage the letter. "It's a Black Spot. It may contain some terrible news."

They huddled around the note, as Anna read the contents aloud.

"To the crew of the *Esperance.* You are to be attacked by Pirates. 4pm Friday."

"That's tomorrow," gasped Shani.

Anna continued.

"Defend yourselves or die! Signed: The Pirates of Rousse (their marks)." Tom and Ian had both put a cross and a smudgy thumb print here, and at the bottom they had written: "PS. Losers buy the ice creams."

This was one of very few moments in their lives, when Anna and Shani were lost for words. They were surprised, shocked even. Did Tom and Ian really have the nerve to spring this on them? Obviously they did. But slowly, their thoughts turned to the delicious possibilities of this declaration of war.

"Well, good for them!" said Anna at last. "War it is then, and we'll give them a jolly good thrashing too."

Shani nodded, wide eyed with excitement , but still unable to speak.

"Bunch of no good pirates!" said Bart. "I knew they were up to something. Well, we'll show them a thing or two."

Just then Mr and Mrs Riley arrived, parked their car overlooking the beach, tooted the horn and waved.

"Right, Bart. I'll have to phone you later, to plan our campaign," said Anna.

"It's explorers against pirates now," said Bart.

Chapter 10

The Pirates of Rousse

Tom and Ian had reached their home port. They put the fenders out and left *Kitty* tied up alongside the pier while they went up to fetch the trailer. As they stepped off the pier they looked up to see a swarthy man with a dark jacket and a woolly hat approaching them. Tom smiled and nodded by way of a greeting but there was no smile in return. The man just pushed passed them in a hurry and walked out towards the end of the pier. Tom raised his eyebrows at Ian.

"Funny sort of a bloke," whispered Tom.

They fetched the trailer down, and pulled *Kitty* up to the hard standing.

"There's just time to do the flag," said Tom. "We'll have to do the rest tomorrow morning."

When they had put the mast up, they hadn't thought to attach some flag halyards, and there was no way to reach the top of the mast to fix an eyelet. There was only one thing to do. The mast had to come down. Tom tapped in a screw eye near the top, and screwed it up tight, then he threaded some cord through the eye, fixed another eye near the bottom to act as a cleat, and tied the halyard loosely to that. They raised the mast up again and secured it in place.

Tom tried out the new halyard. "It would be better with a little pulley wheel at the top," he said, "But that'll do for now."

He didn't try hoisting the flag, as it might attract attention.

"What we'll do, Ian, is, we'll go to the vinery tomorrow to make our weapons," said Tom. "Then we'll finish everything off here, after lunch, and set sail at about half three, to get there for four."

"I wonder if they've found the Black Spot," said Ian, looking over in the direction of the *Esperance*. "I haven't seen any sign of them. I don't know if they're back yet."

Tom looked up and down the coastline on the other side of the bay. Then he looked out to sea.

"Listen to that, Ian. Sounds like someone's in a hurry."

They could both hear the howl of a high speed craft approaching, and then they saw it heading into the bay. A black RIB* which came in at great speed, only slowing down within yards of Rousse pier, where it came to a halt by the steps at the pier head. The two boys watched as the man who had pushed past them earlier threw his bag onboard and climbed in.

"I don't know that boat, do you, Ian?" said Tom.

"No, don't think so," said Ian. "Do you reckon they're off fishing?"

"Yeah. Could be. That's what usually brings people

round here. Really good fishing off the reefs."

"I didn't like the look of that one who just got onboard though," said Ian.

"Yeah. Talk about unfriendly," said Tom. "I can't understand why some people have to go around being all grumpy and miserable like that. Anyway, come on. We'd better be getting back. If we're very careful, we can just have a peek to see if they've found the Black Spot when we collect our bikes."

Tom and Ian took the inland route back to the *Esperance*, and it was only when they reached the Pont St Michel that they had to be more careful, so they would not be seen. They kept a watchful eye out for the others, and tried to keep as low down as possible in case someone was watching from the beach. They reached the clump of bushes where the bikes were hidden.

"Get down!" said Ian, in a sudden urgent whisper. "It's them. It looks as if they've just arrived."

They crouched down in the bushes, and were just able to see what was going on. They watched the others searching the beach, and then Shani pointing at the boat, and Bart retrieving the Black Spot in the dinghy. Then Mr and Mrs Riley arrived in the car.

"Phew, that was close," whispered Tom. "They would have passed us on the road if we'd been five minutes later." They had to stay hidden until everyone had gone. "Oooh! I'm getting cramp in my leg," Ian complained.

Finally the coast was clear, and they were able to extricate themselves from their hiding place.

"Looks like they found it alright," Tom said, gleefully.

"I think it's been a pretty good day's work, Ian. Don't you?"

"Brilliant!" said Ian. "But I can't wait until tomorrow."

The two swashbuckling pirates cycled home together, chatting as they went, about what they might need in the way of weapons.

"How about bows and arrows?" Tom suggested.

"But we wouldn't want anyone to get an arrow in the eye," said Ian. "I know. We could put some cotton wool, or something, over the ends of the arrows, and tie them up with some string, so they would have a sort of padded end."

"That's a good idea," said Tom. "Shall I try and get some cotton wool?"

"No, I'll bring some. Seeing as you'll be providing the wood," said Ian. "It's only fair."

Later that evening, Anna phoned Bart. "Things are a bit tricky," she said. "Mother's playing up again, and we really have to go with them to see some old friends. I'd forgotten it was all arranged. But don't worry Bart, we've told them we have to be down at the beach by 2.30 to go swimming. That'll leave plenty of time for lunch, and then they'll drop us off."

Bart spent a restless night. He was racking his brains, to think of a plan. How was he going to defend the *Esperance* against a swarm of pirates? He knew he had the girls to help him, but he felt responsible somehow for their safety, as well as the safety of his ship, and these responsibilities weighed heavily upon his young shoulders. Tom and Ian had probably been planning their attack for ages. How could he compete? It wasn't going to be easy. But ever so slowly, as he finally drifted off to sleep, a plan was taking shape in his mind.

The next morning found Ian and Tom hard at work at the vinery, which had become a weapons factory, and what a perfect place it was for this purpose. Everything they needed was close at hand. Lengths of wood in all sizes, nails and screws, string, and other bits and pieces, and all of the tools they needed too.

Ian was on the production line for arrows, taking some long sticks from a bundle which Mr Le Page used for tying up his climbing beans, cutting the sticks in two, and tying on the padded ends. Then he finished them off, by cutting a groove in the other end to take the string of the bow. Tom was working on his special invention. A catapult for firing water bombs, which they decided to call "The Cannon."

As they worked, they were practising their pirate voices.

"Ahaaar, Tom lad. Ye be a foin stout fellow, ahaaar," said Ian.

"Avast me hearties. Splice the mainbrace, bejabers," said Tom, getting his Irish mixed up with his Pirate.

Having exhausted their repertoire of pirate phrases, they went back to normal. "What are we going to use to fire these arrows, Tom?" asked Ian.

"Last time my dad made a bow, he used a piece of willow," said Tom. "There's some round the back of the vinery."

They took the saw with them, selected two suitable pieces of willow, and cut them to size. Then Tom cut a groove in each end, and tied some heavy nylon fishing line through the groove at one end. Leaning on the piece of willow to give it a slight curve, he pulled the nylon line tight, jammed the top end into the groove and tied it off. "There. That should work alright," said Tom.

"Looks pretty good to me," said Ian. "Give us the twine, and I'll finish mine off. Then we can try them out."

"Hee hee!" Tom chortled. "We're going to be armed to the teeth, Ian. Armed to the teeth!"

After some target practice with the bows and arrows, Tom finished off the cannon. "It's a good job my dad never throws anything away," he said, looking at the cannon with a critical eye. It was a complicated affair, made up of old bits of wood, galvanised pipe, greenhouse fittings, and some lengths of shock cord, which Tom had found hanging on a hook, all fixed together with used nails and screws, which they had to rummage for in an old cardboard box.

Then it was time for lunch, which was the usual, sandwiches. Tom had cheese, and Ian had corned beef, so they swapped a round each. It was nicer to have some variety, and corned beef was a treat for Tom, as he never had it at home. They finished off with apples and chocolate biscuits.

After lunch they made themselves wooden swords, and Tom made himself a wooden knife. He thought it might look more piratical to leap over the bulwarks with a knife between his teeth. To finish off, they found an old black dust sheet, and cut themselves some black bandanas, and a black shoulder sash each, from which to hang their swords.

"There's only one problem," said Ian. "How on earth are we going to carry this lot on our bikes?"

"That's a good question, Ian," said Tom. "We'll have to manage it somehow. It's too far to walk, and then we'd have to come back for our bikes. Tell you what. If we bundle up the arrows and the swords, I'll carry those, and the bows, and if you can strap the cannon on your back somehow. We've plenty of rope. Oh yes, and we need a handful of those poly bags, and some rubber bands."

After much careful packing, and strapping on, they were so heavily loaded that they only just managed to cycle out of the vinery, and then they wobbled off down the road.

Bart had also been busy that morning. After breakfast, he had written down his plan for defending the *Esperance*. He always found it easier to think about things if he wrote them down. This was how it must feel, he thought, to be a general or an admiral on the eve of a great battle. He wrote down his ideas, and how the enemy might possibly react, and how he would deliver the coup de grace, the final master stroke, which just might save his ship, and his crew, from falling into the hands of those horrible grisly pirates.

After thinking things carefully through, he went down to the boat, and busied himself with the practical arrangements of his cunning plan, and testing everything to his satisfaction. It was a pity the girls weren't there to keep him company, he thought to himself. He could manage without them for the time being, but he hoped they would arrive early enough, so that he could explain everything to them.

Time passed slowly for Bart. Lunch time came and went. Two o'clock, half past two. Still no sign of the girls. Three o'clock. Everything was ready, but where was his crew? The time ticked slowly by. Something must have happened to them. He knew how keen they were to join in the battle. Half past three. Well, he would just have to manage by himself. No time to hang about. The enemy would soon be upon him.

"Bart!" came a shout. Anna and Shani were running down the beach. Bart hopped into the dinghy and pulled himself quickly in to the shore.

"Quick!" he panted. "Jump in! They'll be here any minute, and we have to get ready!"

"Sorry we're late," said Anna. "Lunch went on and on. So, what's the plan?"

Bart and the girls climbed onboard the *Esperance*, while he explained hastily what had to be done. As the first part of the plan, he showed them how, by pulling on one of the mooring ropes, he could move the dinghy back to the shore.

"Right. Now everybody into the cabin, and we must be as quiet as we can possibly be."

Once they were inside the cabin, Bart locked the door from the inside, and they sat quietly waiting for the pirates to attack.

The Pirates of Rousse had launched the *Kitty Kat*, which was now a heavily armed pirate ship. They paddled a little way out from the pier, and then thought they had better try out the cannon. First they had to make water bombs, filling the poly bags with water and tying them up tightly with the rubber bands. The cannon was loaded, cocked back against the strain of the shock cords, and let go.

"Fire!" shouted Tom, "Thwack!" went the cannon, and a second later, "Splash!" went the water bomb, into the sea.

"That's fantastic!" said Ian. "They won't stand a chance."

Tom was as happy as he had ever been. Here he was, pirate captain of his own ship, fairly bristling with weapons, a fair wind, a steadfast crew, the prospect of a sea battle, and a glittering prize almost within his grasp. Tom was in his element.

They hoisted the Jolly Roger to flutter at the mast head, set the mainsail, and ventured forth in pursuit of death or glory (preferably glory). In the distance, they could see the *Esperance*, lying snugly in the corner of the bay.

"She's a sitting duck," said Tom. "What's the time, mister mate?"

"Gone four, cap'n!" Ian replied.

"Well then me hearties, we're going straight in for the kill," said Tom.

Slowly, *Kitty Kat* edged towards her prey, and a brave sight she made too, with her pirate flag, and the pirates

in their bandanas, with their swords and other weapons at the ready. Then they were within range.

"Let's give her a broadside!" shouted Tom. Ian fired a few water bombs. The first splashed into the sea, but the others went "Splat!" against the bulwarks and "Splat!" against the cabin door.

"A direct hit. Well done, mister mate. Now, let's get the sail down and man the bows and arrows," ordered captain Tom.

Several volleys of arrows peppered the helpless ship, but still there was no response. "They must be hiding," said Tom. "Come on Ian, we'll board her."

They tied up alongside, and scaled the bulwarks, Tom with his wooden knife between his teeth, as planned. They tumbled onto the deck.

"Come on you lily livered lot! Come out and fight!" shouted the pirates.

"They must be hiding in the cabin," said Tom. He pounded on the door, and tried the handle. "No, it's locked," he said.

"Here Tom," said Ian. "There's no flag up. And look, the dinghy's up by the beach. That means they're not here yet. Maybe they're late, or maybe they couldn't make it."

"Couldn't make it?" replied Tom incredulously. "Couldn't make it?" he repeated, quite perplexed. "Well this is a fine thing, Ian. We organise a proper battle, and they can't even bother to turn up!" He thought for a moment. "We'll just have a good look around, to make sure."

The two pirates went up forrard under the awning, looking carefully from side to side. Tom looked up at the awning. Something was different about it. It looked like some netting had been fixed to the underside...

It was at this precise moment that Bart released the ropes holding up the netting, and the ropes holding up the awning, and Tom and Ian's world suddenly became tangled and then black. There was a brief moment of realisation as they were enfolded by the net. They struggled to get free, and then the heavy canvas awning was down on top of them.

There were whoops and screams of delight, as their captors fell upon them, and before they could do anything they were tied up into a nice tight bundle. Try as they might, they could not get free.

"Let us out of here! I can't breathe! That's not fair!" the pirates cried out.

"Sit on them, girls. And make sure they don't escape!" said Bart. "I'm going to take down that Jolly Roger, and claim the *Kitty Kat* for our prize!"

"You can't do that! You can't have my boat, you rotten thieves!" cried Tom. "Ice creams was the prize, not boats."

"Ice creams? We never agreed to ice creams," crowed Bart, as he lowered the pirates' flag. "Keel hauling is more what I had in mind, or hanging from the yard arm. That's what they used to do to pirates."

"Oh come on you lot! It's getting hot in here!" the bundle cried out plaintively, its frantic punching and wobbling about having finally subsided.

"Do you surrender?" asked Anna.

"Yes, we surrender," answered the bundle.

"Okay, let them out," said Bart. "I think they've learned their lesson."

It was a hot and bothered, and somewhat sheepish pair of pirates that emerged, after the canvas had been rolled back, and the netting untangled. But Tom was never dejected for long.

"I've got to hand it to you, Bart," he said with a laugh. "You certainly caught us out, hook, line and sinker."

They all shook hands, and made their declarations of peace.

"I know you didn't have much of a chance to use your warship against us," said Bart, "But I think you've made a marvellous job of her."

"Do you think so?" said Ian. "Come on Tom, let's show them how everything works."

"Yes, but first of all, Ian, you and me are buying the ice creams."

"Oh you really don't have to," said Anna.

"Yes, we insist. That's what we agreed, and that's what we are going to do," said Tom firmly. The victors could see there was no point in arguing, so Bart pulled out the dinghy and ferried everyone ashore. They chose their ice creams at the kiosk, and sat down on the beach to eat them.

They discussed what they might do the next day.

"I'm pleased we're all explorers together again," said Shani. "When are we going to sleep on the *Esperance*?"

"I think tomorrow might be okay," said Anna. "The parents are going out in the evening, so we would have been left by ourselves at the hotel anyway. Shall we try for tomorrow?"

"Fine by me," said Bart. "But what about during the day?"

"The trouble is, they keep moaning at us, poor old things," said Anna.

"It's only because they want to spend some time with you, Anna," said Shani.

"If the weather's fine, we could have a day on the beach, and your parents could come too," said Ian bravely.

Anna grimaced. "I don't think a whole day would be a good idea," she said. "Maybe half a day."

"I know what we could do," said Bart. "In the morning, Tom and Ian, you could come around to my gran's house, and then you could phone us there, Anna, and let us know if there's any chance of meeting up later on."

"Okay," said Anna. "And don't forget to bring that book, Bart. The one about the dolmens, I'm dying to have a look at it."

"Seeing as it's Saturday tomorrow, my mum and dad might want to go to the beach as well," said Tom.

"The more parents we can get, the better," said Anna. "Then perhaps they can all chat together about grown-up stuff, and leave us to get on with things."

Everyone laughed at this. "Come on," said Bart, getting to his feet. "I want to have a go with that water cannon before it gets too late."

Chapter 11

Bart's Gran's House

The following day, the weather did not start off too hopefully. It was grey but dry. Tom's mother was optimistic though. "I'm expecting it to clear up later," she told him. "The forecast was fine for later on."

Tom had told his mother about the plans for everyone to meet up on the beach.

"That would be nice, Tom," she said. "Dad has to work this morning, but I was hoping we might all meet up for a picnic lunch, and make a bit more of a day of it. You know how he likes to go to the beach on the weekends."

Ian arrived on his bike, and informed them that his family too were hoping to get to the beach later. Even his older sister, Emma, was going, provided the sun came out.

"I told them Ladies Bay. Is that alright with you, Mrs Le Page?"

"Yes Ladies Bay will be fine Ian. We like it there don't we, Becky? The water's nice and shallow for paddling, isn't it darling?" Becky nodded her head, and continued playing with her doll.

"Come on, Ian," said Tom. "We'd better be getting off to Bart's. See you later, mum. See you, Becks!"

Bart's gran didn't live too far away. Bart had explained where it was, and they had both known the house. It was a lovely old granite farmhouse, set back from the road on a hill. Bart was keeping an eye out for them, and ran outside to meet them.

"Morning, Ian, morning, Tom, come along in. We'll go up to my room, shall we?" he said.

The house was very grand inside, in an old faded sort of a way, and full of character. It felt like it hadn't changed for hundreds of years. On the stone and wood floors were lots of old faded rugs, and on the walls dark paintings of landscapes and old fashioned people, in gilded frames. In the hall, a grandfather clock ticked and tocked in a slow measured fashion as they walked past, and all of the furniture was dark and ancient looking. Tom and Ian weren't used to houses like this.

There was an open door, leading into the sitting room. "I suppose we'd better say hello to gran," said Bart, and he led them in. Bart's gran was sitting at the far end of the room, looking out of the window.

"Gran, these are my friends, Tom and Ian," said Bart.

The old lady turned to greet them. "Hello, Tom and Ian. It's very nice to meet you," she said, smiling warmly at them, although she looked a little dazed, as if her mind had been far away, thinking of other things. "I was just looking at my birds ... out in the garden," she said. "I get so much pleasure from them, you know. They keep me company when Bart isn't here."

Just outside the window, Tom and Ian could see a paved area, with a bird table and a bird bath, and feeding bags of nuts and seeds, hung up to attract the birds. There were several birds, hopping and fluttering about; a blackbird with its yellow beak, a starling with its iridescent plumage, and a couple of sparrows.

"It's the magpies that I don't like," said Bart's gran. "They attack the others. Now, young gentlemen, I don't suppose Bart has even told you what to call me?" Everyone looked uncomfortable. "Well, I'm Mrs Henry. Now, what are your surnames?"

"Le Page," said Tom.

"Domaille," said Ian.

"Those are very good Guernsey names," said Mrs Henry. "Did you know, Ian, there have been Domailles in the Vale parish for at least three or four hundred years, probably more. The Le Pages are perhaps a little more recent."

"This is a lovely old house," said Tom. "Have you lived here a long time, Mrs Henry?"

"Yes indeed I have, Tom. Nearly sixty years. It was my husband's house, and his family home before that, and Bart's father was brought up here. We have many happy memories." She paused for a moment, and smiled again. "Well now. You don't want to be standing around chatting to me. Off you go and play. And Bart, make sure you give your friends a drink, and there are some biscuits in the kitchen."

"Thank you, gran," said Bart, and led them off upstairs,

to see his room.

They reached the first floor landing, where there were more faded rugs on bare floorboards, more old pictures on the walls, and an old mahogany linen press*. The wall facing them was made of vertical wooden boards, painted cream, and in this wall Bart opened a little, narrow, boarded, cream painted door, which they had not noticed at first, and took them up a narrow flight of stairs.

"Cor! It's like a secret door leading to a secret passage," said Tom.

They found themselves standing in a vast open attic area. On one side there were three dormer windows set in the sloping ceiling, and on the other side some roof lights. Again, nearly everything around them looked really old, but in this particular room there were many things which were of special interest to boys.

"This was my father's bedroom when he was young," said Bart, "And there are still lots of his old toys and things here."

There was a rocking horse in the corner, together with some old threadbare teddies and other cuddly toys. There was a ping-pong table, an old train set, a miniature stationary steam engine, some old pond sailing yachts, and, just about the only modern thing, a Scalextric set, all laid out ready to use. It was boys' heaven.

"Wow, Bart, this is fantastic!" said Ian and Tom together, not knowing what to look at first.

"Here. Look at the view," said Bart. "We're really high up, and you can see for miles."

They looked out of one of the dormer windows, from which there was a wonderful view inland, over fields and gardens and rooftops, and through the roof lights on the other side you could see out over Grande Havre to the sea. By now the sun was starting to peep through the clouds, and everything was bathed in a gentle golden light.

"I wish I had a view like this from my bedroom," said Tom.

"So do I," laughed Bart. "At least I get to enjoy it when I'm over here. I'm lucky, really."

Ian admired the view as well. "Isn't that the *Esperance* over there?" he said.

"Yes," said Bart. "You can just make her out. I expect you can see more of her than I can, Ian, as you're so tall."

"Come on, Bart," said Tom. "Let's have a go with the Scalextric!"

After half an hour or so, there was a call from downstairs. "Bart! Telephone for you!"

"That'll be Anna," said Bart. "Stay here. I'll be back in a minute."

Ian and Tom sat on the edge of Bart's bed, to wait for him.

"I feel a bit sorry for Mrs Henry," said Ian.

"So do I," said Tom. "She must get awfully lonely in this great big house when Bart isn't here. And he only comes over for a few weeks each year, and his dad lives in France. I wonder if she has any other children or grandchildren."

Bart came thundering back up the stairs. "It's all fixed," he panted. "Meet up at Ladies Bay at twelve."

"So we'll have to leave in about half an hour," said Ian.

"Yeah. Okay. Shall we go outside for a bit?" suggested Bart.

"Is there anything to explore?" asked Tom.

"Yes, we can look at the old barns, and the quarry," said Bart.

"Come on then," said Tom.

They tumbled down the stairs, and out into the garden. The sun was out, the sky was blue. It was turning into a lovely day.

"Do you think your gran would like to come to the beach?" Ian asked Bart.

"She usually has lunch with a friend of hers on Saturdays," said Bart. "Actually, I don't think the beach is really her thing."

"We could ask her," said Tom. "It's always nice to be invited. Even if you don't actually go. That's what my mum says anyway."

Bart showed them around the barns, where there were still some old bits of farm machinery and tackle, and haylofts to explore. Outside one of the barns were some huge curved pieces of granite, arranged in a circle. The centre of each piece had been hollowed out to form a deep channel.

"That looks really old. What is it?" asked Tom.

"It's an old cider trough," said Bart. There used to be a great big stone wheel, on the end of a pole, and you would have an ox or something to pull the wheel around, and put all your apples in the channel. Then they would be crushed, and you would shovel them up, and all the juice would be pressed out to make cider."

"I reckon Anna would be really interested in that," said Ian.

They walked over to the old quarry, which was right at the back of the property. Like most old quarries, it had filled up with water, which looked dark, and deep, and uninviting.

"My grandfather used to keep a rowing boat in there," said Bart.

They all agreed they would much rather do their boating in the bay.

"I wonder where all the stone went from this quarry,"

said Tom.

"They used to export it all around the world," said Ian. "Well, to London for sure. It was used all over the place where they needed really hard stone, for steps and pavements and things like that."

"And nearly all the old buildings in Guernsey are made of granite," said Tom. "The old forts and Martello towers, and everything. Your gran's house, Bart. I wouldn't be surprised if that was built with stone from this quarry, and the barns."

The boys made their way back to the house.

"Bart, I've just remembered. The book about the dolmens," said Ian, who had been thinking about quarrying, and huge slabs of granite.

"Oh yes," said Bart. "Just as well you reminded me. I would have forgotten again."

They went in through the front door, and into the sitting room. "Gran. You know that book I asked you about? The one about the dolmens? Is it alright if I lend it to Anna?"

"Yes Bart, that's fine," said Mrs Henry. "It's in the bookcase over there. I have plenty of books on local history, including the dolmens, so she needn't hurry to give it back. She can post it back to me if she likes. It's not a heavy book, so it wouldn't cost too much to post."

Bart found the book, and showed it to Tom and Ian.

"Look, there's the one we found the other day, when you weren't with us," he said. Tom and Ian were duly impressed.

"This is just the thing," said Ian, leafing through it.

"Anna will be thrilled with this."

Mrs Henry was pleased by their enthusiasm. "It's not terribly lengthy, but all of the known sites are described in quite some detail," she said. "It really is a little gem."

"Mrs Henry," said Tom. "We're all going to Ladies Bay at twelve o'clock for a picnic lunch. My parents will be there, and my sister, and Ian's family, and Anna, and everyone. Would you like to come with us?"

"Oh, that is very kind of you, Tom. But, I haven't been to the beach for years. I'm not sure I could manage it with my arthritis. As a matter of fact, I usually go out to lunch on a Saturday, but Marjorie phoned this morning to say she couldn't make it. So I am free. Oh I don't know. Do you think I should?"

"Yes. Come on, gran," said Bart. "It would be a nice change for you. We could take a folding chair with us."

"Yes, do come!" said Tom. "It would be lovely to have a crowd of us. The more the merrier!"

"Well do you know, I think I will come," said Mrs Henry. "It would be nice to have a picnic on the beach. I haven't done that for such a long time."

"Shall I make some sandwiches?" asked Bart.

"No, don't bother with that, or we'll be late," said Mrs Henry. "We'll buy what we need from the kiosk. But get me that bottle of sparkling wine out of the fridge, Bart, and we'll need half a dozen plastic cups. That should help the party to go with a swing!"

Chapter 12

The Beach

They gathered their few bits and pieces, and in no time at all they were ready to go.

"Leave your bicycles here, boys, I might as well give you all a lift," said Mrs Henry.

They piled into her little car, which was surprisingly roomy inside, and drove off towards Ladies Bay. As they were driving along Pont St Michel, Bart suddenly had an idea.

"Hang on a minute, gran. Can you drop me off at the *Esperance* please. I'm going to sail around in the dinghy, and meet you all on the beach."

Mrs Henry smiled and nodded. She knew how much Bart loved his boating. He couldn't bear the idea of spending hours on the beach, without a boat to mess around in. They dropped him off, and continued on their way.

"He's just like his father," said Mrs Henry to Tom and Ian. "Mad on boats; and motor bikes and cars. That will be the next thing I suppose, motor bikes."

To get to Ladies Bay, they had to drive a fair way inland, and then back out to the coast, so that they could park nearby. They arrived at the same car park near the tearoom which Mrs Henry frequented with her friends, and where Bart had seen her when they had been exploring. It was just gone twelve o'clock. As Mrs Henry parked her car, Tom saw Mr and Mrs Riley arrive, with Anna and Shani. They were quite surprised to see Tom and Ian getting out of Mrs Henry's car. Tom unloaded the folding chair, and took Mrs Henry to meet the others. Ian carried the rucksacks.

Introductions were made, and everyone was laughing and chatting, when, in quick succession, Ian's family arrived, and then so did Tom's. The noise grew even louder, with more introductions and greetings, and then the whole party descended on the beach. Heavily laden with all of their provisions and equipment, they found a suitable spot, where the sand was nice and dry, and established their base camp.

Ian's sister, Emma, being older than the other children, was a good deal quieter, and settled down daintily on her beach towel to sunbathe. The others split into various groups. The parents and grandparent set about unpacking and erecting sunshades and windbreaks, although there was really very little wind. Anna and Shani had gone all soppy over Becky, and were helping her to build a sandcastle.

"Isn't she just so sweet?" said Anna.

Tom and Ian went down to the water's edge to see if Bart was on his way. They took off their trainers and paddled in the sea.

"There he is, over there! See that brown sail?" said Ian. "He's going to be ages. There isn't much wind, and it's against him."

"Oh, I don't know," said Tom. "He's actually going way faster than we could with *Kitty*."

They saw the dinghy tack on the other side of the bay, and head towards them, close hauled. They watched as the sail was pulled in tight, then let out a bit until it fluttered, then trimmed in again.

"I reckon he'll be here in about ten minutes," said Tom. "Come on, Ian, let's go and see what's for lunch!"

Back at base camp, Mrs Le Page was chatting to Mrs Domaille, who was rubbing sun cream over Emma's back and shoulders.

"Do be careful, dear," said her mother. "The sun is at its hottest now. Ten minutes more and then cover up."

Mr Le Page and Mr Domaille were sitting quietly, looking out to sea and watching Bart's progress in the dinghy, and Mr and Mrs Riley were chatting with Mrs Henry.

Tom was slightly disappointed when he arrived, to see that lunch had not yet been laid out. "Come along, mother. How about some lunch?" he suggested.

"Tom Le Page!" said his mother jokingly. "You and your food!" But she started to take various containers out of one of the bags.

"Jolly good idea if you ask me," said Mr Le Page. "I've been working all morning, and I'm famished."

"If only these women would stop chatting for a

moment, and look after their menfolk properly!" Mr Domaille said, teasing the ladies.

Noticing some activity at base camp, Anna, Shani and Becky left their sandcastle building, and turned up looking hopeful.

"Here, you two," said Mr Riley. "Pass some of these around."

He had ordered several rounds of sandwiches from the hotel, and these, together with similar offerings from Mrs Le Page and Mrs Domaille, were duly passed around by Anna and Shani, who made wonderful waitresses.

"What excellent service! Thank you very much," said Mr Domaille and Mr Le Page.

Bart finally arrived on the beach, pulled the dinghy in as far as he could, and trotted up the beach to meet the others, and to join in the feast. Mrs Henry produced her bottle of sparkling wine, which Mr Riley opened with great ceremony, and it was shared out amongst the adults.

"This is the life!" said Mr Riley. "Champagne on the beach. Now that's what I call living in style."

There was plenty of food to go around, and great variety too, as everyone had brought something different; cheese and tomato, ham and pickle, egg mayonnaise, chicken and coleslaw, even a few smoked salmon sandwiches, which Mrs Henry thought went particularly well with the sparkling wine, and finally cakes and buttered gache. Mrs Henry had wanted to make her contribution of more food from the kiosk, but they were all so full at the end, that she offered instead to buy ice creams later on.

It was a day of great jollity, and everyone seemed to get on so well together. You would have thought the grown-ups had known each other for years. The Domailles and the Le Pages had known each other of course. The others had only just met, but they would leave each other at the end of the day, the very best of friends. Even Emma Domaille, who sometimes found other people irritating, especially her parents, managed the occasional smile and laugh.

This suited the others very well. "Just as we planned," Anna whispered to Ian. "Come on. Let's make a run for it."

The word was passed around, and soon the exploration party was mustered, and marching off in the direction of the rocks, saying they needed to walk off their lunch. On the way, Ian and Tom took a detour with Bart, to help him pull the dinghy in a bit further. "That's the only trouble with this beach," said Bart. "You just can't get in close, because it's too shallow, and you have to wade in and out."

The girls started to clamber over the rocks. Becky had been allowed to join them, and she was having a wonderful time being looked after by the two bigger girls.

"Come on, Becky, hold my hand," said Shani. "Now one foot here, and the other foot there. That's it! We'll make an explorer out of you yet." Becky nodded seriously.

"Hey look over here!" called Anna, who had gone ahead. "There's a really big rock pool!"

The boys had caught up with them by now, and everyone went as quickly as possible to see what she had found.

"I'll go and fetch my shrimping net from the boat," said Bart.

The rest of them gathered around the edge of the pool, then crouched down and peered in, to see what might be in it. There were various kinds of lichens and sea weeds, and different coloured stones and shells.

"Look at that, Becky," whispered Shani. "Some little baby fishes, can you see them? And look at this shell, isn't it beautiful." She reached into the pool, and picked up a large oval shaped shell, which was covered inside with mother of pearl.

"That's an ormer* shell," said Tom. "They're common here, but pretty rare elsewhere in the world."

"My mum and dad like to eat ormers," said Ian. "I think they're revolting."

Bart arrived back with the shrimping net, and they all set to, to see what they could find to catch. They found a sea anemone, some tiny crabs, some minnows and some shrimps, and after examining them all carefully in a bucket, they tipped them back into the pool. But Shani kept the ormer shell as a souvenir.

"I'll put it in my room, and use it as a little dish," she said. "And every time I see it, I will think of this day."

It was warm and sheltered and peaceful in amongst the rocks. The sun had warmed the water in the pool, so that it was quite tepid, and delightful for paddling your toes. They could faintly hear the noise of people laughing and playing on the beach, the sound of the sea washing up against the shore, and the calling of the sea birds.

They had been there about an hour, when Bart suggested it might be time to go. "Tide's coming up," he said, "And we don't want to have to swim back."

It was just as well they started back when they did. By the time they had clambered back the way they came, the sea had surrounded the rocks.

"Oh no!" said Shani. "It's just like you said the other day, Ian. We're cut off by the tide."

Luckily it was only about a foot deep where they had to cross over to get back to the beach. Tom carried Becky, to save her dress from getting wet.

As they reached the shore, there was a shout from further up the beach.

"Hello you lot! Are you coming for a swim?"

It was a swarm of parents in trunks and bathing suits; Rileys, Domailles and Le Pages. It was so hot, the thought of a nice refreshing dip in the sea was appealing, so the youngsters went up, changed into their swimming things, and returned to join the others.

The men had waded out quite some distance to find deeper water. Tom, Ian and Bart went after them. The ladies stayed in the shallows, chatting at the water's edge, and paddling their feet, while Anna and Shani played splashing about games with Becky.

Presently, they were joined by Emma, who had very kindly stayed behind to keep Mrs Henry company, but had been persuaded by Mrs Henry that she would be perfectly fine reading her book for half an hour, while Emma went swimming with the others.

The men were enjoying a proper swim.

"Come on then," said Bill Le Page. "Let's swim out around that bobber over there, and back in again."

Off they went, with Mr Riley in the lead. He had a very steady and deliberate style, which made it look as if he could carry on for miles. The others were, perhaps, faster over a shorter distance, so by the time they reached the bobber, Mr Le Page had taken the lead. Mr Domaille, in second place but tiring, tried to see if he could touch the bottom, and everyone was quite surprised when he stood up, and the water was only just up to his chest.

On finding this out, they all touched down with their feet, and had a rest, except Bart, Tom and Ian of course, who were still out of their depth. They had to carry on swimming, and so they overtook the grown-ups, and came back into the shallows first.

Bart's dinghy, by this time, was well afloat, so they tried to climb in over the sides. This didn't work too well, unless you had someone holding down the opposite side. "It's better if you climb in over the stern," said Bart. "She won't tip over then."

Seeing as they were all onboard they decided they just had to go for a quick sail. Tom and Ian hadn't sailed in Bart's dinghy before, and they were dying to see what it was like.

Bart took three lifejackets out of the locker, passed them around, and once everyone had safely done them up he hoisted the sail. It was a simple balance lug, quite like *Kitty*'s really, except bigger and more triangular in shape, and it was a lovely faded browny red colour. Ian pulled up the anchor, Bart pushed the rudder hard over until

the sail filled, and then they were off. The breeze had picked up slightly, and the little boat slipped through the water at quite a speed. Heading out away from the beach, they passed the three elders.

"Porpoises on the starboard bow," said Tom.

"Hey. Don't leave without us! We want to sail in that boat!" called the porpoises. But they waved cheerfully, as the little dinghy sailed past them.

It was at this moment that Tom realised, however much fun they had had on the beach, there really was nothing that could compare to the thrill of sailing. He understood why Bart had asked his gran to stop the car. There was something about the motion of the boat through the water, bobbing and swaying and scudding along, the smell of the fresh sea air, the sheer adventure of it all.

"Here, Tom, you can have a go if you like," said Bart.

They carefully changed places, and Tom took hold of the tiller, then Bart passed him the mainsheet. He was amazed at the feel of the boat through the tiller. She felt so much more skittish and lively than *Kitty*. The wind picked up in the centre of the bay, and in only a matter of minutes they had nearly reached the pier at Rousse.

"Right. Now we're going about," said Bart. "Nice and gently, Tom, push the tiller away from you. That's it, keep it there."

The boat turned into the wind, the sail flapped momentarily then started to fill on the opposite tack. They changed sides, trimmed the sail, and headed back towards Ladies Bay.

"Pull the sail in a little tighter, Tom," said Bart. "We're

pointing fairly close into the wind."

There was quite a pull on the mainsheet now, and the boat was sailing well, heeling over a touch, and creaming through the water. Ian took a turn at the helm, and he too was impressed at how well she sailed.

"Where did you learn to sail, Bart?" asked Ian.

"The Sailing Trust," said Bart. "I started years ago, in one of those tiny little dinghies on the model yacht pond*. Then they move you up to bigger boats in Havelet Bay, and so on. It's a great way to learn, and of course I've read lots of books about it. Oh crumbs, that reminds me. I still haven't given Anna that book."

"I'll remind you when we get back to the beach," said Ian.

"All set for sleeping onboard tonight?" asked Bart.

"Yes, but we'd better get going I think," said Tom. "We have to fetch our bikes, then go back home for something to eat, and collect our things, before we can come down."

"We could have a meal onboard," said Bart. "Let's all bring eggs and bacon. Enough for the girls too."

"Yeah, that should be easy enough to cook," said Ian. "Have you got a frying pan, Bart?"

"No problem," said Bart. "There's pots and pans, and plastic plates, and knives and forks. We'll be fine."

"Hey, look out for that bobber, Ian!" said Tom.

They narrowly missed it.

"Okay, Ian. Just head straight for the beach," said Bart.

The tide had continued to rise, and they were able to sail almost up to the beach, before the dinghy touched, scraped along and then stuck fast. Bart dropped the sail, took the anchor line out over the bow, and stuck the anchor in the sand, pushing it in with his foot.

While the sailors had been away, the party on the beach had dried themselves after their swim, and enjoyed ice creams, courtesy of Mrs Henry.

"Mmm. These are delicious!" said Shani to Becky. "Now you make sure you tell Tom how delicious these ice creams were, when he gets back," she giggled, "And what a shame it is that they all missed out!"

By the time the sailors returned, everyone had decided it was time to go, and they were busy packing up. Bart arranged with his gran for provisions to be collected by Tom and Ian, and finally handed the book about dolmens to Anna. She was so excited.

"Oh thank you, Bart! Thank you so much, Mrs Henry. I'll make sure you get it back," she said, as she started to flick through the pages.

The parents made final arrangements to ensure that the night crew of the *Esperance* would have all that they needed, and fond farewells were made on all sides. "What a pity you're going back so soon," said Mrs Le Page to Mrs Riley. "I hope we'll see you before you leave."

Ian and Tom helped Mrs Henry up to her car, and carried her chair for her. Then they all drove off, one by one, and tooted their horns as a final goodbye. Anna and Shani went back with Mr and Mrs Riley to their hotel, and Tom and Ian went back with Mrs Henry, to collect their bikes and Bart's provisions. Bart trotted down the beach, and sailed back to the *Esperance* to make preparations for their night onboard. The wind had picked up a little more for his return journey, and the sky was starting to cloud over. Still, he thought, they could not have asked for better weather for a day on the beach.

Chapter 13

Onboard at Night

All the way back to the hotel, Anna's nose had been buried in the booklet which Bart had given her. Its title was: "Prehistoric Monuments of Guernsey." It was crammed with information on the dolmens, although she soon found out that they should not be called "dolmens" at all, because they had more than one capstone. They should be called "megalithic tombs". The sign post on the one they had found at La Varde was wrong too, when it had incorrectly described the tomb as a "passage grave", or so the book claimed.

"Well? What does it say?" asked Shani. "Is it any good?"

"Good? It's fantastic!" said Anna. "There's just about everything in here. Bits of history, and folklore, and all the right names for calling things. Megalithic, Mesolithic, Neolithic ... Palaeolithic..." (she struggled to read out the last one). "They're all over the place. All over the island. But the sad bit is that there used to be loads more, and most of them were destroyed years ago. There used to be ... Hang on where was it." She leafed back through the book. "Ah yes ... 68 tombs and 39 menhirs, that's standing stones. And now there are only ... 15 tombs, and 7 menhirs. Isn't that sad?"

Shani nodded. It did seem sad, all of that ancient history lost, and she could see how important it was to Anna.

Back at the hotel, they had a cup of tea and some biscuits in Mr and Mrs Riley's room, to keep them going until tea time.

"Bart's going to cook us eggs and bacon," said Shani proudly.

"Are you sure you don't need to take anything?" asked Mrs Riley.

"Only nighties and toilet bags," said Anna. "Oh. And maybe our swimming things, just in case."

"Well you're certainly not going swimming at night, young lady!" said Mrs Riley sternly.

But even for Anna, who was really quite adventurous, the idea of swimming at night did not appeal. "No, mother," she said. "But we might want to swim in the morning."

"Well just make sure you wrap up well. Take jumpers. It can be cold on the sea at night."

When they had finished their cups of tea, Anna and Shani went back to their room while Mr and Mrs Riley got dressed to go out.

"They'll probably be ages getting ready," said Anna. She slipped off her shoes, lay down on her bed, and picked up the book again.

"Hey, listen to this, Shani. Apparently, there was this huge dolmen, there are only a few bits left now, and they're actually still there in this school playground. Look at the photo." She showed the photograph to Shani.

"Hmm yes," said Shani, not really that interested.

"Yes, but listen to this. And this is actually true, Shani." Anna read from the book: " 'A man, called Mr Hocart, decided to break it up, and he used the stone to build himself a house, and' ... listen to this ... 'disastrous consequences followed ... As soon as the house was completed, it burnt to the ground, and two servants perished in the flames' ... Then he tried to export some of the stone in two vessels ... 'in which he had a financial interest, and both vessels were lost at sea'."

Shani sat, transfixed, as Anna continued.

"Then he went to live in Alderney ... 'and his house there was destroyed by fire'... Then he decided to return to Guernsey...'but during this voyage, a part of the rigging broke, fell on his head, and fractured his skull. He died immediately'."

During the telling of this tale, Shani's mouth and her eyes had opened wider and wider. "That can't be true!" she gasped.

"Oh yes it is," said Anna. "Look here." she pointed to a sentence, and read it out. " 'Sir Edgar Mac Culloch personally made an investigation.' You see. It's perfectly true."

"Well," said Shani. "I don't know if I want to go into any more of these tombs, or dolmens, or whatever you want to call them. If you do any more exploring, you will have to be very careful not to disturb anything."

"Absolutely. We don't want to invoke the wrath of the ancient gods," said Anna, feeling very explorer like. "Just imagine though. He was really cursed. Just like the curse of Tutankhamen, or worse. Mind you, he asked for it. It says here that everybody warned him, but he took no notice ... And each time the hammer struck the stones, you could hear it a mile away... Oooh! Pretty spooky, don't you think?"

"I wonder if the children play on the stones," said Shani, looking at the picture in the book. "It looks like they're right by the school building."

"I shouldn't think the gods would mind children playing on them," said Anna.

Tom and Ian had collected their bikes from Mrs Henry's house, and Ian had carefully put in his rucksack the half a dozen eggs and rashers of bacon she had given them.

"It has been a lovely day," she said. "Now mind you come and see me again. And thank you ever so much for inviting me."

She waved them off as they rode down the gravel drive, and through the gateway.

"Shall we drop the eggs and bacon off on the way?" suggested Ian.

"We won't actually drop them, Ian," said Tom, messing around as usual. "We'll hand them carefully over to Bart. No, actually that is a good idea, because we've loads of stuff to bring back later on: sleeping bags, and more food, and drinks and stuff."

They saw Bart as they were cycling along the Pont St Michel. He had just arrived on the beach, and was busy rolling up the sail, and tidying the dinghy. They pulled up by the kiosk, and walked down the beach.

"Hi, Bart. Here's the eggs and bacon," said Tom. "I'll get some more from my mum, and then there should be plenty for all of us."

"Great. Thanks a lot, Tom. I reckon we might need a nice hot meal. It's getting a bit chilly," said Bart.

"It's a shame it's clouded over," said Ian. "I hope it's not going to rain."

"I'll go and light the stove," said Bart. "That'll warm up the cabin anyway, and I'll be ready to start cooking as soon as you and the girls get back."

"I can't wait!" said Tom. "I'm really looking forward to sleeping onboard."

"Come on then, Tom," said Ian, who also couldn't wait. "The sooner we pick up our stuff, the sooner we can get back."

They picked up their bikes, and cycled home. Tom peeled off at his house, and Ian continued along the lane. "I'll be back as quick as I can, Tom!" he called out.

Mrs Le Page had been preparing a list in her head, of all the things that Tom might need. It was one of her main aims in life to ensure that her husband and her children would never go short of anything she could provide.

"Ah, Tom," she said. "I was just thinking about you. Now, I've put out the eggs and bacon, and also you're going to need some bread and butter, and what about a few tomatoes? And perhaps some marmalade for breakfast, and you'll need some milk, and some cocoa, or tea bags?"

"That would be great, Mum. I think Bart has tea bags. Some cocoa would be nice though. But how am I going to carry it all, and my sleeping bag, and my toothbrush, and I'm taking my bathers as well, in case we go for an early morning swim."

"An early morning swim?" said his mother. She couldn't really see Tom going for an early morning swim, but she decided to humour him. "I'll get your dad to give you a lift," she said.

Ian returned after about half an hour, his rucksack stuffed to bursting.

"My goodness me!" said Bill Le Page. "Where is it you're going? The North Pole, is it?"

"You never know," said Tom. "Once we get onboard, we might decide to up anchor and sail the seven seas."

"Well you certainly seem to have the equipment for it," said his father, as they set off.

They were soon on the beach again. Bart helped them to carry their things down to the dinghy, and ferried them across to the *Esperance*. By this time, the Rileys had arrived in a taxi, and Bart had to quickly row back to fetch Anna and Shani.

"Now have you got your mobile phone? Do be careful, and phone us anytime if you need us," said Mrs Riley. They waited in the taxi until the girls had climbed onboard, and then everyone waved as the taxi drove off.

Alone at last! The explorers could hardly believe it. It seemed ages ago that Bart had first suggested sleeping onboard, and after all the persuading of parents, and all the planning and arranging, they had finally achieved it. Now they had all of the evening to look forward to, and then a night onboard. There was a moment of silence, then everyone was chattering at once.

"We've done it!" said Bart.

"Isn't this great!" said Anna. "Way better than a stuffy old hotel room."

"I don't know what to say!" said Shani. "It's just so exciting!"

"Yes, isn't it!" said Tom. "When are we going to eat, Bart?"

Everyone laughed.

"Let's all go and warm up in the cabin, and I'll make a start," said Bart.

The cabin looked ever so inviting. The stove was burning brightly, and two lanterns had been lit, giving a cosy glow, one hanging from the ceiling, and one standing on the worktop by the sink. Everyone filed in and took their places, while Bart and Ian laid out the provisions on the worktop. Ian sliced and buttered the bread, while Bart took an old black frying pan, which had been warming on the stove, and fried first of all the bacon, and then the eggs. Wafts of delicious cooking smells filled the cabin. Ian sliced the tomatoes, put them onto some plates with the buttered bread, and passed each one in turn to Bart, who served up the eggs and bacon.

"Eat while it's hot," said Bart, and they were all so hungry, they didn't need telling again.

"This is absolutely delicious," said Shani.

"Well done, Bart. Well done, Ian," said Anna.

Ian's mother had provided an apple tart for afters, which they left for a while to warm on top of the stove, and then they polished it off with some Guernsey cream. There was hardly a scrap left, which made washing up so much easier afterwards.

By the time they had finished clearing up it was starting to get dark.

"Let's tell some stories," said Tom.

"Do you mean ghost stories?" said Ian, in a spooky voice.

"Yes. If you like."

"I know a good story," said Anna. "I just found it today, in that book you gave me Bart."

She told them the story of the poor unfortunate Mr Hocart, which they all found quite scary, but also very interesting, as it was about real people and places on the island that they knew.

"What else have you found in the book, Anna?" asked Ian. "Are there any other dolmens we can explore? I wouldn't mind having a look at that one at La Varde, which Tom and I didn't see."

"Because you were too busy being pirates," said Shani cheekily. "And then we went and discovered La Varde Dolmen, and we discovered that awful man in the old ruined fort, didn't we Anna? Just goes to show how much better explorers we are."

"What man in the fort?" asked Tom.

"We met this man in some old ruins on the headland, and he was really nasty to us, wasn't he Bart?"

"Yes, and then he went off, and the next thing we heard this engine start up, and we went to have a look, and he just belted out of the bay in this black inflatable."

"That's funny," said Ian. "We saw someone getting onboard a RIB at Rousse pier, didn't we Tom?"

"Yes. This bloke just pushed past us on the pier. Looked like a real misery guts. He didn't say a word, just barged us out of the way. Then this RIB came in, absolutely flat out, and the guy just hopped in and off they went."

"Sounds like he was nearly as rude as the one we met," said Anna. "I should think they would get on really well with each other. Anyway, we were talking about dolmens, and I know we shouldn't call them dolmens, but it's much easier than the other words. There is apparently another dolmen, according to the book, which is one of the most important ones in north-west Europe, and it's at a place called Paradis, in the Vale."

"I know where that is," said Tom. "It's near the Beaucette Marina."

"Is it too far to walk?" asked Anna.

"No. I reckon we could do it," said Bart.

"Yes. We could go most of the way across the common. Then the last bit we could walk through the lanes," said Tom. "It would make a fantastic expedition."

"I reckon it would take us an hour and a half, or two hours maybe," said Ian. "So that's three or four hours, there and back."

"Why don't we do it tomorrow," suggested Anna.

"I don't know if we'd have time," said Ian. "We have to go to church in the morning, and we don't get out till about twelve. Then there's lunch."

"Yes it would be a bit tight," said Anna, "And the parents will probably want us to do something with them. Well let's try and do it on Monday. That's our last day, and Bart's, so we'll just have to do it then. If we can keep all the parents happy tomorrow, and the grandparent, sorry, Bart! Then they'll just have to let us go on our expedition on Monday"

They all agreed that Anna's plan was the best way to proceed, and then went back to their story telling. Bart told them about a time when he had gone into a German bunker with some friends.

"I was in this dark passage. Pitch black it was. But at the far end of the passage was a doorway, brightly lit with sunlight. Then all of a sudden this black shape appeared, coming towards me. It was like a black square shape, blocking out the light at the far end, and as it came towards me it sort of tilted and wobbled from side to side, so you could just see the light around its edges."

"What did you do?" asked the others.

"I turned and ran out the way I had come in, as fast as I could go," said Bart. "I never found out what it was, and I didn't want to either!"

Then it was Tom's turn.

"I remember one night, when I was late getting home. I've told Ian about this, haven't I, Ian?" Ian nodded. "I was riding my bike along the lane from Ian's house," Tom continued, "And, you know that lamppost on the corner, Ian? Where that other lane branches off towards the common? Well under the lamppost there was an old couple just standing there. I thought to myself, well what are they doing there just standing still, under the lamppost, at night? And as I got closer, I saw they were wearing really old looking black clothes, and they were just standing there, not moving, not speaking. I didn't say a word to them, and they didn't say a word to me. There wasn't a sound. I cycled past. They didn't look at me, they just kept looking straight ahead. It wasn't frightening at the time. It was just strange. I had never seen them before, and I have never seen them since."

"Woooh spooky!" said Shani. "Sounds like ghosts to me."

And so they went on with their stories, and after half an hour or so they were all feeling slightly nervous, and Shani decided to change the subject.

"It's going to be lovely and warm, sleeping in the cabin," she said. "I hope you boys will be alright under the awning."

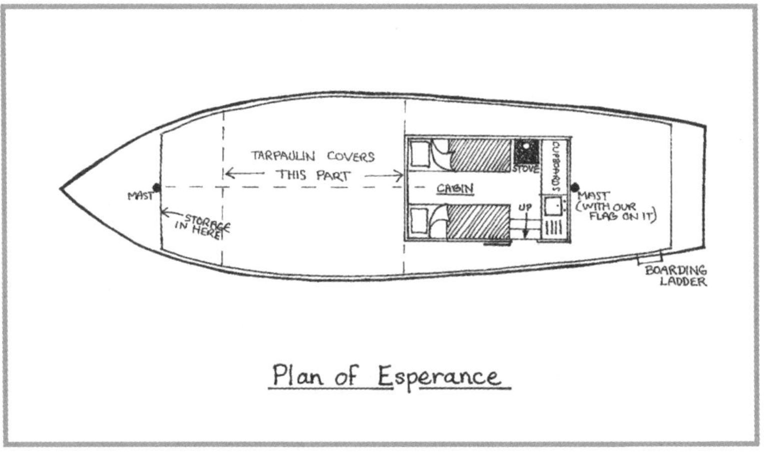

Plan of Esperance

Bart seemed confident enough, but to Tom and Ian, the idea of leaving the cosy cabin and venturing out into the cold dark night, was starting to seem less attractive. If the weather had been warmer, it might have been different, but it was getting decidedly cold and windy out there. Still, they didn't want to look like cissies so they kept their thoughts to themselves.

The evening continued and the explorers carried on chatting about so many things. Anna, Bart and Shani told Tom and Ian about the old ruins near Fort Pembroke, and Tom and Ian told the others all about Mr Le Page's vinery. They talked about their various schools, but didn't dwell on this subject for too long. They were on their holidays after all, and they didn't need to be reminded of school.

"So which church do you go to?" Shani asked Ian.

"Tom and I both go to Delancey," said Ian.

"But that's not its proper name," said Tom. "Its proper name is 'Our Lady Star of the Sea.' "

"Oh. What a beautiful name!" said Shani. "I think I would like to go there too."

"It is a lovely name, but it's only a little church," said Ian.

"Was it built by the fishermen?" asked Shani. "It sounds as if it might have been."

"No, it was the men who worked in the quarries," said Tom. "We used to export a lot of stone from Guernsey at one time, and quite a few quarrymen came to work here, and they needed their own church."

"We don't go to church," said Anna.

"Neither do I," said Bart. "Only sometimes with my gran."

"You should try it," said Tom. "It's really nice. You get to meet lots of people, and say hello to everybody, and we usually have a game of football or something afterwards, and drinks and biscuits in the hall."

The evening drew on and everyone was growing more and more tired.

"Come on, guys," said Bart, eventually. "Let's go and get our beds ready. All hands on deck."

They left the girls to settle down in the cabin, took one of the lanterns, and made their way out along the deck towards their sleeping quarters. To start off with, the wind was not blowing directly in under the awning, and the bulwarks provided some additional protection, so they were able to arrange the camp beds in a relatively sheltered place.

"Once we get into our sleeping bags, we'll be as snug as anything," said Bart.

They got undressed as quickly as they could, leaving on their pants and tee shirts, and dived into their sleeping bags to keep warm. The wind changed to a more westerly direction, and blew now more directly under the awning, causing it to flap up and down. Bart blew out the lantern. It was pitch black. They couldn't see anything, but they could hear the sea breaking against the boat and on the shore, and they could feel the boat rising up to meet the waves.

"I've never known it as rough as this in the summer," said Bart. "It's usually as quiet as anything."

"We're never going to get to sleep with all this racket," said Ian.

Tom snuggled down into his sleeping bag. He tried pulling it up over his head to muffle the sounds of the sea and the creaking and groaning of the ship's timbers. That's better, he thought. But then he heard another sound, a low thrumming and burbling. He popped his head out and sat up to listen more intently.

"That sounds like an engine," he said. "Listen. Can you hear it? There's a boat out in the bay somewhere."

"Oh come on, Tom," said Ian. "I'm trying to get to sleep."

"No one's going to be out in this weather," said Bart.

"I'm sure there's something out there," said Tom. "I'm going to have a look."

He wriggled out of his sleeping bag, pulled on his jumper, and felt his way up forrard. There was quite an up and down motion as the bow of the little ship rose and fell with each wave. He held on to the bulwarks and peered out into the bay, listening for the sound of the engine. There it was again, carried on the wind, and now he was quite sure it was an engine. He could hear it getting closer, a powerful outboard motor running at very low revs, just ticking over. He could see virtually nothing in the darkness, only the white foam of the waves breaking around the Esperance. No lights then. It sounded close enough that he was sure he would see it, if it had its navigation lights on.

Closer still it came, then the engine stopped and he was sure he could hear voices, then nothing. He stayed listening for a few minutes but there was no sight or sound of anything.

"Come on, Tom. What are you up to?" called Ian.

He made his way carefully back to his bed.

"There was a boat out there," he said. "I'm sure of it."

Ian yawned and smiled to himself.

"You're mad. Tom. Who's going to be out there at this time of night?"

"I thought I heard something too," said Bart. "Maybe it was a car on the headland."

Then it started to rain. Slowly at first, they heard a gentle patter of raindrops on the awning, in stops and starts, then heavier. There was a loud drumming against the canvas of a sudden squall and then it faded away.

"Is it stopping?" said Tom. Then there was a distant rumble.

"Oh no. That's all we need," said Bart. "A thunder storm."

By now it was way past their normal bedtime, and they were beginning to think perhaps they should have stayed at home, tucked up warm and safe in their own beds. But at the same time they couldn't help feeling excited, being out at night, in a boat, in a thunder storm. The thunder rolled again in the distance, then there was a flash of lightning, and for a split second, everything around them was lit by a brilliant white light.

Bart started to count, "One, two, three, four."

Then came the thunder clap and rumble.

"That means it's four miles away," said Tom. "Pretty close."

Then the wind came back with a roar. The canvas billowed and flapped around them. And with the wind came the rain, a heavy downpour, hammering on the canvas and bouncing up from the decks.

"We're going to get soaked!" cried Ian.

The girls, in the meantime, had managed eventually to fall asleep. At first they had chatted for a while on various topics: their holiday, what a good chef Bart was, the cabin and how cosy it was, what they might do tomorrow, which shops might be open on a Sunday, and other things. They had talked about the proposed expedition to the stone-age tomb, and the book about the tombs. Then they changed into their night clothes, cleaned their teeth and had a wash, and climbed into their bunks.

"It doesn't sound very nice out there," said Shani, listening to the wind. "I hope the boys will be alright."

" They're probably enjoying it," said Anna. "I wouldn't mind sleeping out there myself, if it was a bit warmer."

They settled down in their bunks, and enjoyed the muffled sounds of the wind and the sea, and the gentle motion of the boat tugging at its mooring ropes. Then Anna blew out the lantern, and they said "Good night," and after ten minutes or so, they finally drifted off.

Shani dreamt she was on a merry-go-round, sitting on a dappled grey mare, which went up and down and round and round, and the music was a strange mixture of whistling and wailing and crashing and drumming noises. What was best about her dream was that Anna and Tom, and Bart and Ian were all there as well, riding on different things, and laughing, and everyone was having a happy time.

Poor Anna's dream was not so pleasant. It started well enough. She was on an expedition with the other explorers. They were all properly kitted out with khaki shorts and shirts, and pith helmets. Then suddenly she got lost, and couldn't find the others. The land around her was very much like L'Ancresse Common, and she was walking up and down over little hills and hollows. She reached the brow of a small hill, and looked down into a dip where a tribe of stone-age men were having a picnic. The leader of the tribe was wearing some terribly torn and tattered overalls. He turned to look at her and she saw it was the man from the old ruined fort. He was angry at being disturbed, and he shouted at her in savage language. Then he shouted at the others and they picked up their weapons and came running towards her. She turned and ran, but they carried on after her.

At first she thought she could out run them, but then they seemed to be gaining on her. There were arrows swishing past, and falling all around her. Then she came upon a wooden hut, and she ran inside and bolted the door behind her. She was surprised to find that by rushing into the hut, and slamming the door, she had woken Shani, who had been asleep in a bunk, in the hut.

"Anna!" called out Shani.

Then the savages were upon them, pounding on the door and shouting:

"Let us in! Let us in!"

"Anna!" shouted Shani.

"Let us in! We're getting soaked out here!" shouted the savages.

"Anna! Wake up!" shouted Shani. "Quick, it's the boys!"

Anna awoke with a start, and stumbled out of bed towards the door. "Oh thank goodness!" she said, still half asleep. "Thank goodness we've been rescued." She unlocked the door, which immediately blew open. Cold air and rain blasted into the cabin, and in fell three very wet and bedraggled boys.

"Ooh look. It's raining men!" giggled Shani.

"It's alright for you two!" Bart shouted above the noise of the storm, as he wrestled the door shut. "We've got soaked. The awning's blown off and everything."

"I hope *Kitty*'s alright," said Tom, remembering they had left her on the beach.

"She'll be okay," said Ian. "The tide must have gone down quite a bit now. She's probably high and dry."

"Never mind *Kitty*. Will you all stop shouting please. I've got a headache," said Anna, still trying to grasp what exactly was going on around her.

"Sorry, Anna," said Bart. He felt for the matches, managed to find them, and lit the lantern. He looked at Anna, and could see she was not quite herself. He looked at Ian and Tom, shivering and wet through. He was starting to feel it was his fault that everyone had got into this mess. "Sorry, everyone," he said. "It was my stupid idea for us to spend the night onboard. I am sorry."

"No, Bart. It's not your fault," said Anna. "Come on. Let's all sit down and decide what to do. Here. Use our towels to dry yourselves off. What's the time?"

"Oh no," gasped Ian. "It's half past two. We're not going to get any sleep at all at this rate."

"Do you think you should phone your parents?" Shani asked Anna.

"No way!" said Anna. "They'd go berserk if we phoned them at half past two in the morning, and we'd never be allowed to do anything at all, ever again." Anna was starting to feel less groggy, and she knew that she had to rise to this challenge. "Right. What we'll do," she said, "Is... you and me Shani, can sleep in this bunk, and two of you boys can sleep in the other bunk, and one of you will have to sleep on the floor."

"I'll sleep on the floor," said Bart, still feeling as if he was partly to blame.

They sorted out the driest of the sleeping bags, and put that on the floor for Bart, and he found an old blanket in the cupboard to cover himself with, and a spare pillow for his weary head. Before too long, they were all nodding off. The *Esperance* had taken the ground, the storm was abating, and they were all just so exhausted that, cramped as they were, they went straight to sleep, and continued to sleep soundly through the rest of the night.

Chapter 14

The Morning After

Bart was the first to wake up. He looked at his watch. Six o'clock. Oh dear, only three and a half hours sleep. Through the portholes of the cabin, shafts of sunlight shone in, catching tiny fragments suspended in the air. He watched them dreamily for a moment or two, then tried to gather his thoughts. The first thing he should do, he thought, was to go up on deck and check for damage. He quietly rose to his feet, picked up some of the wet clothes and sleeping bags lying around and about, and crept silently out of the cabin and up on deck.

It was a beautiful morning. So quiet. No traffic on the coast road, no people on the beach. It felt for a moment as if he was the only person in the world. The sky was blue, the sun was shining, and everything around him was fresh and bright and colourful.

"A new day," he said to himself. "A brand new day."

He looked around the boat. No damage to speak of, not that he could see. *Kitty Kat* was safe, above the high tide mark. The dinghy was lying alongside. She seemed fine, except she needed bailing out. It was a good thing they had rolled up their sails, and tied things down properly, he thought.

He spread out all of the wet things to dry in the sunshine, and then went looking for the awning. With all of the flapping about, it had come undone along one side, and had been blown over the other side, into the water. Luckily the remaining ropes had held fast, so he was able to gather it up, and leave it to dry over the bulwarks. The camp beds had been blown about, but were still onboard, and there was really no damage at all that he could see. Thank heavens for that, he thought. Perhaps things were not quite as bad as they might have been.

He stayed up on deck to avoid disturbing the others. Best leave them sleeping as long as possible, he thought. Then he decided he might as well make himself comfortable on one of the sun beds, while he waited for the others to come to. Before he knew it, he had fallen asleep again.

Anna was the next one to wake up, about an hour later. She had been sleeping on the outer side of the bunk, so she was able to slip out without disturbing Shani. The others were all still fast asleep. Just as well, she thought. She could get dressed, and start sorting things out, before anybody's parents arrived. They had to make it seem as if their night onboard had been perfectly safe and uneventful.

She slipped on her clothes, and suddenly realised Bart wasn't there. He must have had the same idea, she thought. Very quietly, she crept up the steps and out through the cabin door. What a beautiful morning, she thought, as she emerged into the warm sunshine. She looked about her, and smiled as she caught sight of Bart sleeping peacefully on the camp bed. Then she saw the wet things spread out to dry in the sun, and she started to turn them over, so that they would dry evenly on both sides.

By this time it was nearly eight o'clock, and Anna's mother could contain herself no longer. She had spent a restless night, tossing and turning, and worrying about the two girls. Mr and Mrs Riley had returned to the hotel at about midnight, after a very pleasant evening out with their friends. The taxi had dropped them off right by the main entrance doors, but even then they had to run in to avoid getting soaked by the rain. The taxi driver had not helped matters. "The Peninsula?" he said. "It's going to be rough down there tonight. These summer storms are the worst, you know. Could be a few boats washed up in the morning."

"Oh Edward! What are we going to do? Those poor children, out in a storm, on that wretched old tub. I think I should phone Anna, to make sure they're safe."

"No, darling. Not at this time of night," said Mr Riley. "Most likely they'll all be fast asleep, and you'd only wake them up. Leave it till the morning. I'm sure they will be perfectly safe. The boat is in a very sheltered spot, and I believe she has been moored there for years, so there really is no need to worry."

Mrs Riley had been slightly comforted by these words,

and had reluctantly agreed to wait until the morning, but she had hardly slept a wink, and now it was nearly eight o'clock and she could wait no longer.

Bart was woken by the ring tone of Anna's mobile.

"Yes mother, it's me ... Yes, we're all fine thank you ...Yes, it was a terrible storm, but we're all okay ... Some of our things got a little bit damp, but we've put them out to dry in the sun. Isn't it a beautiful day? ... Yes, but don't come too soon, we haven't had breakfast yet ... As late as possible please ... Alright then, see you about half nine ... okay, bye." She put the phone down and turned to Bart. "Did you get that, Bart? We've got till half past nine. We'd better wake the others, and get breakfast on the go."

"Alright," said Bart. "I'll get the stove lit. Come on, you lot!" he called, as he went down into the cabin. "Show a leg! Breakfast time!"

Ten minutes later, the crew were dressed and up on deck, looking a little bleary, but apart from that, none the worse for wear.

"What's for breakfast?" asked Tom.

He was greeted by the usual mixture of groans, laughter and disbelief.

"You don't think of anything else, do you, Tom?" said Shani.

"Oh yes I do!" said Tom. "I think about bikes and cars and boats...." He paused and looked out across the bay. "That reminds me. Any sign of that boat I heard last night?"

"What boat?" said Anna.

"Tom thinks he heard a boat out in the bay last night," said Ian, "But we think it's fairly unlikely in that sort of weather."

"Yeah. Probably a car I should think," said Bart, "Out on the headland. The wind can play funny tricks with noises like that."

"No, it was definitely an outboard motor," said Tom. "I would know that sound anywhere. It didn't sound like a car engine at all."

"Well there was no sign of any boat when I got up at about six," said Bart, "But maybe I'll have a scout around later on."

"That's not a bad idea, Bart," said Anna. "What if it was those nasty types in that RIB? I had a really bad dream last night, and that awful man from the old fort was in it. It could have been a warning."

"Anna!" laughed Shani. "It was only a dream!"

They had breakfast up on deck, sitting on the camp beds in the fresh air. They finished off the loaf of bread, with butter and marmalade. Then they had cereal, and by the time they had finished that, Bart appeared with mugs of steaming hot cocoa. "It's really good, this cocoa," he said. "You only have to add hot water and give it a stir."

After breakfast, Bart hopped down into the dinghy and bailed her out, so she would be ready to take the others back onshore.

"It's been a wonderful adventure, sleeping onboard," said Shani. "Even if we are all a bit tired."

"Yes. It's been great" said Bart. "I'm really gutted I

have to leave on Tuesday. There's all sorts of other things we could do."

"So are we," said Anna. "We'll all have to keep in touch, and arrange to meet up again as soon as we can."

"Never mind," said Tom. "We still have all day tomorrow, and I'm really looking forward to the expedition."

They all cheered up a little at this thought.

"I hope we manage to find it," said Anna, referring to the dolmen. "It's supposed to be quite a special one."

"We'd better leave ourselves plenty of time," said Bart. "Shall we try and meet up earlier? Say nine o'clock?"

Everyone agreed to meet at nine. They cleared away the breakfast things, and packed up their sleeping bags and towels and other bits, which had all dried out nicely in the sun.

"Pity there isn't time for a swim," said Tom. "My dad will be picking us up soon, if we're going to make it to church on time."

Sure enough, Bill Le Page was the first to appear in the car park by the kiosk, and he gave them a wave.

"See you tomorrow!" said Tom and Ian.

Bart took them back to the beach, and returned to collect Anna and Shani. Soon everyone had gone, and Bart rowed back to the *Esperance* by himself. He sighed to himself. It was probably the tiredness, but he couldn't help it. He just felt miserable that he was soon to be parted from his new friends. "Come on," he said to himself. "It's no good getting silly about it."

He rested on his oars, and looked around him at the beautiful bay, and the old ship waiting patiently for his return. "I'll just have to try and be like you," he said to *Esperance*. "We'll have times apart, and times together, and we'll just have to make the best of it."

After he had finished tidying up he walked around the beach to Rousse Pier and back but there was no sign of the RIB, nor of any other boat with the kind of motor which Tom thought he had heard.

Bart spent the rest of the day with his gran, and she was delighted. She took him out to lunch at his favourite restaurant, overlooking the marina at Beaucette, and afterwards they bought the Sunday papers, and a sailing magazine for Bart, and went back home for a good old read. Mrs Henry talked to Bart about her childhood, and all the people she used to know. She had some fascinating tales to tell.

Just like Bart, Anna and Shani, particularly Anna, hated the thought of being parted from the others. "Wouldn't it be lovely if you could buy a house and we could come here to live?" Anna suggested hopefully to her parents.

"Yes it would be lovely, dear," said her mother. "But we couldn't entertain it at the moment. We do love the island, but your father just has to be in London, for his business. All of his clients are over there, and his contacts."

"Business, clients, contacts," said Anna later to Shani. "What a lot of nonsense!"

"You have to be realistic, Anna," said Shani. "What about my family? They couldn't all come over here. It's the same for all of us."

"Well, at least we'll get to come back on holidays," said Anna. "You will come with us again, Shani, won't you?"

"Of course I will, if I can," said Shani. "I've had a lovely time, and I wouldn't have missed it for anything."

They spent their day driving around the island, and stopping off at various places of interest. They stopped for a late lunch at a gorgeous little café, right on the beach, and afterwards they went for a long walk on the south coast. It was completely different scenery from the north of the island, with high granite cliffs and little sheltered coves and fishing harbours, quite perfect, they thought, for a bit of smuggling.

"There must be caves and tunnels and all sorts down there," said Anna, as they walked along the cliff path.

"Just like Phil the fisherman told us," said Shani, remembering their Herm trip.

"Yes, and I've been thinking, Shani. You know what Phil told us about the smugglers, and that awful man who was in my dream, and his nasty friend, and Tom hearing their boat in the night? I'm sure it was their boat, and I can't help feeling they are up to something. There's something about it that doesn't feel right."

"You think they might be smugglers?" said Shani. "But no one has seen them doing any smuggling have they? We haven't any proof of anything have we?"

"I suppose not. Perhaps it's because he was so awful to us. I can't seem to forget about it. It's probably just me."

Tom and Ian met up after church and made various arrangements for the following day.

"We could really do with some binoculars or a telescope," said Tom.

"My dad's got a little telescope," said Ian. "I'll see if I can borrow it."

"Ok then," said Tom. "So that's compass, chart, telescope, Anna will bring the dolmen book and her sketch pad, Shani will bring the map, and we'll need plenty of provisions to see us through the whole day. It's going to be a long hike."

Chapter 15

The Great Expedition

At nine the next morning the explorers started to arrive at HQ. Somehow, things were not quite the same as usual. Anna was in a good mood, because this would be their longest and most exciting expedition yet, and at the end of it, hopefully, they would explore the Dehus Dolmen, described in the book as one of the most important archaeological sites in Northern Europe. The others were not quite so happy. They couldn't help thinking this was to be their last day together, and there was something of a gloomy atmosphere hanging over them. This wasn't helped by the weather. The skies were overcast, and it had started to drizzle, that very fine drizzle that sticks to your clothes. They looked about them and everything was grey; the sky, the sea, the weathered stone of the old church of St Michel du Valle, and the granite cottages and walls stretching along the grey tarmac road. Even the trees, drooping under the weight of the drizzle, and the wet grass and gorse of the common were a sort of greeny grey.

"Come on, you lot!" said Anna, as they set off along the road to Les Amarreurs. "You'd think we were off to a funeral or something!"

She had guessed what was on their minds and did her best to cheer them up.

"This is our longest expedition yet. We might find something quite amazing at the end of it, and there's lots to see on the way. We're going to show you two pirates what you missed when you went off scheming and planning your dastardly deeds, and there's loads of towers and forts to explore as well."

Tom and Ian immediately cheered up when they remembered their pirate adventure, and the thought of the old forts, with possibly the opportunity for a bit of swashbuckling, also appealed to them.

"What I can't understand is ...," said Tom, "This fort here on my chart is called Fort Le Plomb, but everyone calls it Fort Le Marchant."

They all gathered around to inspect the chart, which Tom had cleverly folded and put in a clear plastic bag, so you could see just the parts you needed to without the chart getting wet.

"That is odd," said Shani, looking at her map. "Look. It's shown on the map as Fort Le Marchant, and there's some tiny writing underneath. I wish I had a magnifying glass. Oh, I think it says Rifle Range."

"That's right," said Ian. "My uncle goes rifle shooting there. He's always called it Fort Le Marchant, and my dad. But my dad said, years ago, there was another fort built on top of the old one, which the Germans used for target practice, and it was pretty well wrecked, so they pulled it down in the end. Maybe one of them was called Fort Le Marchant, and the other one Fort Le Plomb?"

"It's a mystery," said Tom. "But whatever it's called, I reckon it must be the furthest north you can go. It looks like that on the chart."

"We should call it the North Pole!" said Shani, quite excited about the idea of visiting the North Pole.

"Yes. This could be an expedition to the North Pole," said Tom.

"Only we need to carry on after that," said Bart. "That's only about half way to the Dehus."

Everyone had cheered up considerably by this time, and they reached Les Amarreurs, where the road turned inland to cut across the common.

"I think we should start off with a bit of exploring right now," said Anna. "It won't take long and it's more or less on our way. I want to have a quick look at this other dolmen near the Fuselage. It can't be too difficult to find. It's in the book. It's called the Hotel or something like that."

They gathered round while Anna consulted the book.

"Does it show anything on the map?" Bart asked Shani.

"Let me see," said Shani, closely inspecting the map. "Yes. It shows the Fuselage, and on the other side of the red blob it says La Platte Mare Cist."

"It says in here," said Anna, "That it's near the sixth tee box on the golf course."

"On the map, it looks like there might be a path leading to it," said Bart. "Look. See where it shows that square bit marked PF. That must be the playing field over there, with the goalposts, and it looks like a path leads off from the playing field."

"Okay," said Anna. "We'll take the path where it's signposted for the Fuselage, then we'll head off east until we cut across the path from the playing field."

As they marched purposefully along the road, the drizzle was easing off and the sky was starting to brighten up. They reached the signpost, and as the explorers set off into the bush, Tom broke into song.

"Exploring we will go, exploring we will go, hey ho the merry oh, exploring we will go!"

Luckily, the others were treated to only one verse.

Soon they came to a path leading off to the east, towards the playing field. From time to time they could just see the goalposts in the distance, over the top of the gorse. The path twisted and turned and they could see that they were getting closer and closer to the main road.

"There must be a turn off to the left somewhere," said Bart.

Eventually the path bore around to the left, and ahead of them they could see a raised square of carefully mown grass.

"That must be the sixth tee!" said Anna, rushing off towards it.

The others arrived to find her stooped over a granite stone embedded in the tee box.

"According to this, it's number nine," she said. "We must have come way too far."

"I don't think the map is very accurate," said Bart.

"Look, there's lots of paths leading off from here. If we just head towards the Fuselage, it's got to be somewhere around here."

They chose a likely looking path, which took them through many twists and turns before it finally ended up on a green, where some young men golfers had just arrived.

"Excuse me," said Anna to one of them. "Do you know of any ancient burial sites near here?"

"Yes. There's one just over there," said the young man, pointing with his golf club.

The explorers wandered off in the direction shown, and immediately found themselves back at the Fuselage.

"This is crazy!" said Ian. "We're just going round in circles."

"It's got to be here somewhere," said Tom. "Come on. Let's take this path here. It's one we haven't been on yet."

The others followed him around a corner, and suddenly found another tee box. Tom looked at the number. Yes it was number six, but where was the burial site? He climbed up onto the tee box to get a better view, and as he looked around him he saw to the north, another tee box, and then to the left of that, a huge piece of granite sticking out of the gorse. "That's it!" he shouted. "Look! Over there! That's got to be it."

When they got to the other tee box, they found that it too was numbered six, and sure enough, right alongside it they found the tomb, L'Autel des Landes. It looked more or less like a shelter, built of massive stones, and open on one side.

"It's a bit small for an 'otel," Tom joked.

"Well, I'm jolly pleased to have found you at last," said Anna to the stones, and she took out her drawing book to make a few notes and a quick sketch.

Bart was starting to feel a bit restless. "Come on, Anna," he said. "We'd better get going. We've hardly covered any ground yet, and it's gone ten o'clock."

"Yes alright, Bart," said Anna. "I've nearly finished. Would you boys like to decide which way we go from here? Are there any short cuts we can take, to make up for lost time?"

The boys consulted the map, and decided to cut across the common towards the Chouet road, then take the road to Pembroke Bay, where they could take the coastal path around the northern coast.

"There's a path that goes all the way up through the gorse from here," said Ian. "So we won't have to worry about getting hit by golf balls."

Although they had enjoyed their exploring, with the grass being still wet, most of them had wet shoes, and it was something of a relief when they finally got back on the footpath which ran alongside the main road. The drizzle had stopped, and the sun was shining weakly through the clouds, so they were able to take off their waterproofs and stuff them into their rucksacks.

"Oh blast!" said Anna, rummaging around in her rucksack, "I think I've left my phone behind. Now I'm for it. If mother tries to phone I'm in deep trouble."

"Shall we go back for it?" said Ian.

"No. We're running late as is," said Anna. "We'd better just get on."

About halfway along the final stretch to the beach, they came across a sign and a path for La Varde Dolmen, which Tom and Ian had not yet seen.

"Well it was much more fun finding it from the other direction," said Anna. "But seeing as we're here, and we need to make up time, we may as well go by the tourist route."

"I don't really want to see it again," said Shani. "I think I'll carry on to the beach, and wait for you there."

"Okay, Shani," said Bart. "I've already seen it too, so I'll come with you. We'll wait for you others on the sea wall."

"Fair enough," said Anna. "What about you, Tom and Ian? Do you want to have a look? It is one of the biggest on the island you know."

"Well if it's that big, we've just got to have a look," said Tom. "Come on then. Race you to the top!"

Tom and Ian raced up the path, hotly pursued by Anna, while Bart and Shani walked off towards the beach.

The three explorers were quite puffed by the time they got to the top of the hill. "Wow! Great view ... from up here," Tom gasped, drawing in great gulps of air.

They quickly found the dolmen, and before they went in Anna read out some of the information in the book. "It was only in the eighteen hundreds that they found these dolmens," she said. "Look. The photo shows it completely uncovered. They must have covered it up since then, because you can hardly see it now. It says here they found skeletal remains, vases, beakers, remains of about 150 urns! Fragments of bronze, and a few stone objects, and it's 33 feet long!"

They crouched down slightly to avoid bumping their heads as they walked into the tomb.

"This is amazing," said Ian. "It's like a proper underground room, once you get in. I wonder where they put the bodies and where they put all the urns and stuff?"

"If you think about it," said Tom, "All those things left in the dolmens must have been for the people who died, for them to use in their next lives. So it must mean they believed, after they died they would have another life, somewhere or other."

"Yeah, that's right," said Ian. "A bit like the pharaohs and all that, in Egypt."

"Yes, and the Vikings, with Valhalla," said Anna.

"I wonder if the Romans and all the others believed in life after death," said Tom. "What do you reckon Anna?"

"Well, most people still do," said Anna. "I know I do. Sometimes I can feel the spirit world. Specially round here."

"Woooh! Spooky!" said Tom. "Come on. I think we've seen enough."

"I can't understand why we've never noticed it before," said Ian, as they emerged. "We've been up here lots of times."

"Yes, but we usually go and play in the bunker over there," said Tom. "Come on, let's have a quick look at the standing stone while we're here."

They looked at the stone, and then quickly showed

Anna around the bunker, which was kept locked, but you could walk around on the top and admire the view. They could see almost all of the common, and the bays on either side, and a good part of the island stretching out to the south.

"It's such a shame we don't have time to look at more of the dolmens," said Anna. "We haven't even seen the ones at Sandy Hook, which is just over the road from the hotel, and there are loads and loads of them all around the island."

"Well, there's always next time," said Ian. "Come on. We'd better not keep the others waiting."

"We can run down over the common. That will save some time," said Anna.

They trotted down hill, following the way that Anna, Bart and Shani had used when they first approached the dolmen from Pembroke Bay. They crossed the fairway and ran down over the undulating hills and hollows till they reached the coast road.

"That was a bit of a bumpy ride!" laughed Tom, as they reached the bottom. "If it wasn't so wet, we could have done some roly-polys down some of those dips."

"There are the others," said Ian, pointing over towards the sea wall.

While Bart and Shani had been waiting for the exploration party to catch up, the sun had come out from behind the clouds, and they had taken off their trainers, and put them to dry on the sea wall. Shani had not been to Pembroke Bay before, so she and Bart had walked down across the sand to the water's edge, paddled their toes, and enjoyed the peace and quiet of the beach. They had the whole place to themselves, except for someone they could just see in the distance at the other end of the bay, exercising a couple of dogs.

"Might as well make the most of it," said Shani. "Back to London tomorrow. There won't be any beaches there."

"Yes. I'm sad to be leaving too," said Bart. "I'm really going to miss you guys."

"Never mind. You're going to France aren't you? To see your father. Where does he live in France? Is it nice?"

"Oh yes. I like France," said Bart. "It's a beautiful place, and the people are really friendly too, but you have to speak to them in French. They don't think much of you if you just speak English. My father has an apartment in St Malo, in the old walled town. It's really nice, with a fabulous view over the estuary. Boats coming and going all the time, and they have some really lovely old sailing boats, like the pirates used to have, and some super-fast racing yachts. It's my second favourite place after Guernsey."

"Wow! That sounds really nice," said Shani.

"Yes. It is nice," said Bart, "But sometimes I wish I didn't have to go from place to place. You know, travelling here, then staying over there, then back to England. Sometimes I wish my family wasn't split up all over the place."

They walked back up the beach, and had just returned to collect their shoes, when the others arrived. Tom told them all about what they had seen and done.

"Right," said Bart. "Time we were heading off. It's

nearly eleven o'clock."

"Time for elevenses?" suggested Tom hopefully.

The others didn't have the heart to say no, so everyone had a quick bite and a drink before they continued on their way.

"Look, there's a café over there. I'm going to see if there's a phone. I really must contact mother to let her know I don't have my mobile with me," said Anna. "It won't take a minute. Then I won't be worrying that she's trying to contact us, and not getting through."

As Anna walked over to the café, the others looked around to get their bearings for the journey ahead.

"I think I can see Fort Le Marchant," said Tom. "Look. Right over there, beyond the headland of this bay there's another headland with something on it. I think it's the fort."

Ian pointed his telescope at the far headland. "Yes it is," he said. "I can just make out one of the target numbers to the right of it, so that must be the rifle range."

Anna returned from the café.

"Any luck?" asked Bart.

"Yes. She wasn't best pleased," said Anna. "But I think I've got away with it. I had to promise to be back by five, or they'll send out a search party."

Chapter 16

The Coastal Path

Duly refreshed, they set off along the coastal path, the beach on their left, the common on their right, and the path stretching out before them, with a number of Martello towers along the way, standing like soldiers, stiffly to attention, guarding over the bay.

"I can see one, two, three ... four, counting that one on the headland," said Tom.

"Yes," said Shani, looking at the map. "Towers number 7, 6, 5 and 4."

"This beach would make an ideal landing place," said Ian. "So that's why they put so many towers along here. To fight off any invaders."

"That one over there has a flag on it," said Shani, pointing to Tower No5.

Ian looked through the telescope. "It's the Guernsey flag," he said. "Red cross of St George, with the golden cross of Normandy on top."

"When you look back at Tower No 9, you can see how much it's leaning over from here," said Shani.

"Cor. It's like the leaning tower of Pisa," said Tom. "If it leans any more, people might come from all over the world to see it."

They marched past towers 7 and 6, reached the end of the beach, and followed the path around towards the tower with the flag on it. As they approached, they could see that the tower was set up on a little hill, just inland of the path. They felt they just had to take a closer look. After all, it was the only tower they had seen flying the Guernsey Flag.

The tower was pretty much like all of the others, except for the flag on top, and a nicely painted staircase leading up to a stout front door. To the side of the door was a plaque, and they gathered round to read it.

"Oh, it's privately owned," said Anna.

"It's a pre Martello Tower," said Ian. "I suppose that means it was built before the proper Martello Towers."

"During the American War of Independence," said Shani, reading from the plaque. "When the French took sides with the Americans. So the towers were built to keep out the French and the Americans. Just as well. Imagine if you and Ian spoke like Americans, Tom."

"That wouldn't be so bad," said Tom. "We could have a ranch, and be cowboys and Indians."

"Privately owned," said Anna again. "It must be wonderful to have your own Martello Tower."

"Pre Martello Tower," said Ian.

"I wonder if there's anybody home," said Shani.

They had a good look around, but couldn't see any signs of life, so they set off again on the path towards

Fort Le Marchant. After they had gone just a few yards the path divided into two, and there was some discussion as to which one they should take.

"It looks like they both meet up again further along," said Shani, looking at the map.

"Well I'm sticking to the coast," said Tom, and Bart and Ian agreed with him.

"You boys take the coastal route then, and Shani and I will go inland," said Anna. "That way we can be sure we won't miss anything. We'll meet you at the fort, if not before."

So the boys turned left and followed the coast, and the girls turned inland.

The coastal path swung down and around a small headland, where there was a tiny little old stone building with a stone roof, which Ian thought must have been built about the same time as the pre Martello Towers, and then the path ended abruptly, facing a steep rocky ridge. It looked as if the ridge had been quarried at some time, as the slope was covered with loose stone and scree.

"Oh no. We may have to go back," said Ian, as they looked around for a way out.

"Hang on," said Bart. "Look, there's a bit of a path up there. It must go somewhere. Let's try it."

They scrambled up the rocky slope, and after slipping backwards a few times on the loose stones, they finally made it to the top, where they were greeted by a fine view of Fort Le Marchant, and an easy path leading down to a pebble beach and then up to the fort. In front, and to the right of the fort, were the large painted numbers of the targets on the rifle range, with a steep bank of sand behind them to catch the bullets.

"Come on, lads!" said Bart. "We have to beat the others to the North Pole!"

They ran as fast as they could, and managed to reach the fort before there was any sign of the girls. Quite out of breath, they staggered up the steps leading to the battlements, and then turned around to look for Anna and Shani. Sure enough, there they were, walking in quite a leisurely fashion down the main pathway to the fort. Even from a distance, they could see that the girls were happily chatting to one another as they strolled along, quite unaware that they had lost the race to the Pole.

"That's girls for you," said Tom.

The fort was built in the shape of a semi-circle, with five gun emplacements which must have been for revolving guns, as there were semi-circular metal tracks behind each post on which the guns had been mounted. There was a wonderful sea view on all sides, which the boys were admiring just as the girls finally arrived to join them.

"What's that black and white tower out there?" asked Anna.

"It's not on the map," said Shani.

"That's where my sea chart comes in handy," said Tom. "Look there see? There's a little picture of it. It's the Platte Fougere beacon, and that's its actual position, there," he said, pointing to the chart. "Look at all the rocks around it. I bet it must have caused quite a few shipwrecks before the beacon was put there."

"What are those letters and numbers underneath?" asked Shani. "L Fl. WR. 10s 13m 16M?"

"Let's have a look," said Bart. "My father taught me how to read those. Now let me see. Right. That means it has a light, with a long flash, white and red every 10 seconds, and the beacon is 13 metres high, and you can see the light from 16 miles away."

"Cor! That's really good, Bart," said Tom. "I've been wondering about that. See, most of the beacons have those letters and numbers. So, that one there, Roustel, QK. Fl. 8m 7M. What does QK mean? Is that quick flashing, eight metres high, and seen from 7 miles away?"

"Yes, that's right, Tom," said Bart. "And those other letters there, Bn Tr. BW. I think that means it's a tower beacon, and it's painted black and white."

"Oh, I get it," said Tom. "Thanks, Bart. I thought it was something like that, but I wasn't quite sure."

"So this is it. The furthest north we can go," said Anna.

"Yes. Well done, everybody!" said Shani, and she went around shaking hands. "Congratulations all round for reaching the North Pole!"

Everyone shook hands with everyone else, and they all felt a great sense of achievement in having gone this far on their great expedition.

"I can see our next objective over there," said Bart, pointing across the bay to Fort Doyle on the next headland. "Come on, everybody. We'd better keep going."

"Okay," said Ian. "But let's have a look at the targets on the way. It's really interesting to see how they work."

They climbed down from the fort, and headed over to the targets on the rifle range. The actual targets had been stored away, but the metal frames and pulley systems for hoisting and lowering the targets were there, tucked away behind a sturdy concrete shelter and embankment, which protected the people who did the hoisting and lowering. A few yards beyond the targets was a great heap of sand which caught the bullets.

"Otherwise the bullets would go whistling out to sea, and kill the poor fishermen, or sink their boats," said Shani.

Tom looked at the steep sandbank, noticing a slight depression behind each target where the bullets landed. He wondered how far the bullets went in before they stopped. He pulled Ian to one side, and whispered in his ear. "Come on, Ian. Give us a hand to dig up a few bullets."

"You can't do that ,Tom. I shouldn't think it's allowed," Ian whispered back.

"Oh come on! I'm only going to dig up a few, and I'll put the sand back afterwards, just as we found it."

Somewhat reluctantly, Ian followed Tom up the sandbank. He looked about to make sure no one was watching them, or shouting at them to clear off. Ian felt very uneasy about this idea of Tom's.

The others were busy inspecting the target holders, to see how they worked.

"I think, after the bullet has hit the target, they mark up the score on the back bit, and then they pull the target down, and that sends up the back bit so the shooter can see what he scored. Then they put a marker in the bullet hole and send the target back up again. Or something like that," Bart was saying.

"Right. So you push down on this side, and the other side goes up," said Anna.

Up on the bank, Tom was carefully digging away with his pen knife, and Ian was still feeling uneasy. He felt very exposed up there. He imagined the bullets thudding into the sand bank, and shivered to himself. After what seemed an age, Tom found what he was hoping for. Some of the bullets were hopelessly torn and twisted, but he had managed to find five which were reasonably straight. They looked a bit like sharks' teeth, with pointy ends, but of course, as they were metal, they were not white but a pinky yellow colour, like copper.

Tom carefully put back the sand, and pressed it into place with his foot. He and Ian, who was very relieved that they had not been caught or shot at, returned to the others.

"Here," said Tom, handing out the bullets. "We'd like each of you to have one of these, as a sort of keepsake."

The others were quite surprised, and delighted.

"Thanks, Tom. Thanks, Ian. That's really cool," said Bart.

"I'm going to keep it with me, as a good luck charm," said Shani.

"We can use them as a secret sign of our tribe," said Anna.

"I reckon they'll polish up nicely," said Tom.

Having conquered the North Pole, and received their

mementoes, the expeditionary force embarked on the next leg of the journey, towards Fort Doyle.

The coastline around the north of the island was wild and windswept. The first bay they came to had a huge mound of pebbles and stones along its length, above the high tide mark, thrown up by the winter storms, and various items of flotsam and jetsam.

"Which is which?" asked Anna. "Is flotsam the stuff that is thrown overboard, or is it the other one?"

"I think flotsam is wreckage which just floats ashore, like that old plank over there," said Bart. "Jetsam is the stuff that's thrown overboard, like that plastic bottle. If you think about it, it sounds like jettison. You know, when you throw something out."

They continued along the path, enjoying the peace and quiet, the beautiful scenery, and the fresh sea air. There was not another person to be seen. On the inland side, they passed a derelict vinery, which was in even worse condition than Bill Le Page's. One of the greenhouses had collapsed completely. In the others, there were more panes of glass out than in, and the timbers were all twisted and bent. Behind the greenhouses four very old and rusty water tanks stood on stilts, each one leaning a little more to the left, so that the fourth one had nearly fallen over.

"They're falling over like a pack of cards," said Tom.

"Or like dominoes," said Shani. "Why did they put those tanks on stilts, Tom?" she asked.

"That was for watering the crops," said Tom. "You see that old windmill there? That would pump the water up from the well into the tanks, and being high up, that would give a nice strong flow of water, so it wouldn't take all day to do your watering."

Pretty soon they reached Fort Doyle. At first they thought it might be closed. The gates appeared to be padlocked, and there was a notice on the wall, but as they approached they could see that the notice was just to tell visitors about the fort. Then they saw another way in. A flight of stairs led down and around, then up through another doorway. When they reached the battlements they were treated once again to a fabulous view over the rocks and sea around the north of the island. The Platte Fougere was now a little closer, and they could see the island of Alderney in the distance. Around to the east they could see Herm and the large rocks off its northern end. Closer to, they had a good view over Beaucette Marina, and then just beyond that something which they had not expected, and over which they became quite excited: a tiny island which looked to be just about a hundred yards off the Guernsey coast, and beyond that but closer inshore, what appeared to be another island.

Chapter 17

The Secret Islands

"I didn't know there were other islands here," said Anna.

"Aren't they beautiful!" said Shani.

"Yes, aren't they quite something?" said Bart. "This is one of my favourite parts of Guernsey, especially this side of Bordeaux Harbour. It's just so lovely and unspoilt. It's a part of Guernsey which is still a bit wild and magical."

Ian and Tom said nothing at first. Tom was dreaming of desert islands, and pirate ships, and buried treasure. They knew about the larger island in the distance, but strangely they had never noticed the smaller island, probably because they had never seen them from this angle.

Tom consulted his sea chart. "It's called Homptole," he said.

Shani was looking at the map. "It's here on the map!" she said, "But it's called Homeril, according to this. I never noticed that before. But I can't make out the name of the other island. It's been covered up by this advert for the Freesia Centre."

"It's called Houmet Paradis," said Ian.

"Paradis?" exclaimed Anna. "That must mean paradise! Paradise Island. Oh we must have a closer look. Come on. How do we get to them?"

"I've never actually approached them from this side," said Bart. "I don't know if the path goes all the way around."

"The map shows a path most of the way," said Shani. "It starts just the other side of Beaucette Marina."

"Come on then," said Anna, quite forgetting about forts, and even dolmens. "Come on. We just have to get a closer look at Paradise Island, and Humpty Hole or whatever it's called. I don't think many people can know about them, because you can't see them from most places. They can be our secret islands!"

So without even looking properly over the fort, or looking at the very interesting plaque showing how the cannon were mounted and telling the history of the fort, the explorers were led off at quite a pace towards the other side of the marina, where they hoped to rejoin the coastal path.

"Mmmm!" said Tom as they passed the kitchens of the Marina Restaurant, and the wonderful cooking aromas wafted out. "Must be getting near lunchtime."

"Well we don't have time for that just now," said Anna. "We'll get to the islands first, and then we'll stop for lunch."

They caught a glimpse of some of the boats moored

in the marina as they passed by.

"Mostly plastic gin palaces," said Bart. "But there's one or two quite interesting. I had a look yesterday when I came with my gran."

On the other side of the marina, they followed a path heading in the right direction, and came to a yard area where several boats had been hoisted out for work to be carried out. There were one or two workmen and their vans, but no sign of the coastal path. The yard was surrounded by a low earth bank, and Tom climbed up on it to have a better look, but he couldn't see anything that looked like a path.

"It's clearly marked on the map," said Shani. "It must be here somewhere."

"Well I can't see it," said Tom.

"It's no good," said Ian. "We'll just have to go back and take the road."

They walked a little way back towards the road, and then they noticed an overgrown gap in the hedge. On the other side, leading towards the sea was a track, which looked as though it had not been used for some time.

"It doesn't look much, but it's our best bet," said Bart. So they took the track, which led them down onto a shingle beach and then stopped. At the top of the beach was a low earth bank, which had a very rough single file path along the top of it. Where there was no path they had to walk along the shingle until they reached a grassy headland where there was a fine view of Homeril.

"Shall we stop here for lunch?" suggested Bart. "It is half past twelve."

But even Tom wanted to go on until they could see both islands clearly.

The path from the headland led them back onto a narrow lane which came down to the coast and then doubled back on itself and led inland and up a hill.

"This must be the lane that leads to the dolmen," said Shani, studying the map. "See, there's the headland. This must be Mielette. We have to go up the hill and round to the right."

"Yes, it is Mielette," said Bart, who had found a sign at the top of the footpath which led down onto the beach. He read from it: "Mielette. The constables warn that swimming in this area is dangerous, due to strong currents."

"So this is where we have to head inland," said Anna. There was a note of reluctance in her voice, because she still had not seen Paradise Island properly.

"Oh come on!" said Tom. "Let's not take the road just yet. I want to get a closer look at Houmet Paradis."

"The trouble is, Tom," said Bart, "We're running out of time, and there's no way round from here. See, the path stops according to the map, and we have to take the lane."

"Well let's at least have a look from the beach," said Tom, so pleadingly that the others could not refuse. And anyway, they were all just as drawn towards the islands as Tom was.

They walked down past the notice onto a pretty little beach covered in pebbles. As they walked down they noticed that many of the pebbles had been worn flat by the sea.

"Cor! These would make really good skimmers," said Tom.

Bart looked up at the cliffs forming the headland between them and Houmet Paradis. "I don't see any way around that," he said.

"Oh come on, Bart!" said Tom. "This is proper exploring. Much more fun than going by road. Let's have a look down there, and see if we can get around at the foot of the cliffs. The tide's going down now, so it'll be quite safe."

"Okay," said Bart, "But we mustn't waste too much time on it."

Tom and Ian went on ahead, down to the foot of the cliffs, where the sea had receded, leaving a thick carpet of slippery green seaweed. They had to tread carefully, as they couldn't see what was underneath. The cliffs towered above them. The waves splashed up against the black rocks, worn smooth by the constant pounding of the sea. It seemed as if Bart was right. There was no way through.

Then Tom spotted a chasm, a narrow opening, partly hidden by the rocks, with steep sides and carpeted floor of green seaweed. Could it be the way through?

"I think I've found it!" he shouted.

The others caught them up, and they all clambered carefully over the slippery rocks and seaweed, and through the chasm, which led them to a secret, sheltered cove.

"Well done Tom!" said everyone.

"Incredible!" said Bart. "I never would have guessed this was here."

"Thank you everyone!" said Tom bowing triumphantly, "And now, I think it's time for lunch!"

They found a cosy nook, higher up the cove, where they were sheltered from the breeze, and had a fine view of both of the islands. The long journey and the fresh air had made them hungrier than they realised, and they soon polished off all of the sandwiches, crisps and chocolate bars they had brought with them, and finished off with drinks and some fruit.

Tom was just finishing his banana, when he heard a faint buzzing noise, like an angry bee, now and then accompanied by a slap...slap. He looked around to see where it was coming from. The noise grew louder, and then he realised what it was: a boat with an outboard motor, running at high speed. He looked out to sea, and in the distance he could see something approaching, way out, north of Herm. Now the others could hear it too.

"What's that coming Ian? Can you see it through the telescope?" asked Tom.

Ian looked out to sea, and aimed his telescope in the direction of the spot on the horizon.

"It's some kind of powerboat," he said. "Having a bit of a rough time by the sound of it. Caw, she's not half moving though!"

The angry buzz of the engine grew louder, and the boat drew nearer.

"I reckon it's a RIB," said Ian, keeping the boat in view through the telescope. "Where on earth has she come from? She seems to be heading this way."

"There's nothing out there, except Dielette* perhaps, or maybe they've come from Cherbourg," said Bart. "Pretty funny way to come in though, and why are they coming in here? They should clear Customs if they've been to France."

Within minutes, the RIB had careered across the entrance to the Little Russel*, and darted in between the two secret islands at full tilt.

"They must be mad," gasped Ian. "They just missed those rocks by inches!"

Suddenly, the RIB swept around and came to an abrupt halt. The engine was cut.

Instinctively, the explorers crouched down out of sight. Ian kept his telescope trained on the RIB, in which were two men wearing wetsuits.

"This is a bit strange," said Bart quietly. "Why have they just come blasting across and straight into this little cove? I think we'd better keep down, everybody. I'm just not sure what they're up to."

With the engine switched off, they could hear the men talking to one another, but they could not quite make out what they were saying. They were looking about them, as if to see if anyone was watching, then one of the men lifted a large grey box out of the boat and dropped it over the side.

"What on earth..?" whispered Ian. "Oh I see... there's a bobber attached to it."

The two men were laughing now, as if at some kind of joke.

"Blimey!" whispered Ian. "I'm sure it's the RIB we saw at Rousse. They've just dropped a box overboard."

"Let's have a look," whispered Tom. He took the telescope and trained it on the RIB. "You're right Ian. I'm sure it's that misery-guts and his mate. Hang on. Keep down everyone! They're looking this way!"

Tom quickly dropped down and handed the telescope back to Ian. "I reckon they might be smugglers," he said. "I've heard about this. They drop something off in a quiet cove somewhere, then they come and pick it up later, after they've been through Customs. Or someone else picks it up."

"Yes! We've heard about that too, haven't we, Shani?" said Anna.

"Surely they can't be!" said Shani. "Are you sure it wasn't just a crab pot Ian?"

"No. It was definitely not a crab pot. It was a solid box, made out of metal, I think."

"Maybe they could be scientists or something," said Shani, "And that box might have equipment in it, for measuring things on the seabed."

"They don't look like scientists to me," said Ian.

"Let me have a look," said Anna.

She took the telescope and focussed it on the boat. "Good grief!" she said. "It's that horrible man we met in the ruins. Yes, I'm sure it is him, and that's his boat. Well he's no scientist that's for sure. Did you say it was a metal box they threw overboard? What colour was it Ian?"

"It was grey, I think," said Ian.

"That's it," said Anna, dropping back down again. "I

knew it. I knew they were up to something, all that whizzing about, and trying to scare us off, and carrying boxes to and fro. They must have taken that box over to France, filled it up with goodness knows what, and now they're dropping it off here, as bold as brass."

Ian took a turn with the telescope. "They're just chatting at the moment, and smoking cigarettes," he reported. Then the engine was started, and after a few minutes the RIB headed off again at full pelt.

But this time they cut it too fine. There was a sudden loud "Crack!" The engine raced for a moment and then died as the boat came to a halt. They could hear the men cursing and swearing. One of them shouted at the other one, blaming him for hitting the rocks. The boat drifted for a moment. Then the strong current started to take them northward and the two men had to paddle like mad towards Houmet Paradis. Fighting against the tide, it took them some time, but they finally made it, disappearing from sight behind the north-west point of the island.

The explorers were shocked.

"What shall we do?" said Shani.

"It can't be anything else," said Anna. "They must be smugglers. There's no other explanation."

"They probably use the ruins to hide whatever it is that they're smuggling!" said Bart. "That's why he was so annoyed when we peeked inside. And when I heard him on the telephone he said something about doing a job on Monday. Maybe this is the job he was talking about."

"I think we should get the police," said Ian.

"Drat! If only I had my mobile," said Anna.

"Hang on everyone. Shush!" said Tom. "I think I can hear them again. Keep down!"

They all ducked down and listened intently. They could hear nothing except the sea breaking on the rocks, a seagull mewing, and the distant putt putt sound of a fishing boat.

"Whatever they're up to," said Ian, "They seem like pretty nasty types, going by the language they use. We're going to have to be extremely careful. We'd better keep well out of their way."

"Do you think one of us should go and fetch some help?" suggested Bart. "I'll go, if you like, while the rest of you keep watch."

"I think we should all stay together," said Ian.

"Well, we can't go back the way we came," said Tom. "They would see us for sure. Even one of us walking back along the beach might be enough to make them suspicious. Perhaps we should just wait here and let them make the first move."

"If we could go the other way they wouldn't see us," said Bart, "But I don't know if it's possible to get through."

"Looks like they're staying put for the moment," said Anna, as she peered carefully around a rock at the island. Then, through the telescope, she spotted something which made her heart leap. Slowly making its way through the channel outside Homeril punching against the tide, was a little red white and blue fishing boat.

"It can't be...Shani...Yes it is!" said Anna. "It's *Cobo Alice*. It's Phil, Shani, Phil the fisherman!"

"Oh my goodness!" said Shani. "Do you think we can stop him? Do you think he will help us?"

"Of course he will help us," said Anna. "He'll know what to do, and he's a pretty big bloke. I don't think they would be too keen to tackle Phil."

"We've got to be quick," said Ian. "Goodness knows what they'll try next."

Anna looked around the rock again. *Cobo Alice* was now almost level with Houmet Paradis, but would pass it well offshore.

"Come on then," she said. "We'll make a run for it. The tide has dropped a bit more now. I reckon we should try and get around the rest of the headland. They won't see us if we go that way and keep our heads down. Then we can run along the beach, and if we all wave like mad Phil is bound to notice."

"Okay," said Bart. "We're not doing any good here."

"Yes, but we've seen what we needed to," said Tom. "Those smugglers are not going to get away with it."

"That's the spirit, Tom!" said Anna.

Keeping as low as possible, and using what cover the rocks provided, the five of them ran, jumped, climbed and scrambled their way, as quickly as they could, around the headland. They reached a rough stony beach on the other side, and looked about to get their bearings.

"Still no sign of them," said Bart.

Cobo Alice was now powering along the channel towards Bordeaux Harbour.

"Right everybody. Start waving those arms about!" said Anna.

They climbed up onto the path skirting around the top of the beach, and ran as fast as they could go. Steadily onwards chugged *Cobo Alice*. On and on ran the five explorers, waving their arms and jumping about as they went.

"Over here, Phil!" mouthed Anna. "Over here! ...Oh blast, he hasn't seen us."

They reached a small parking area, used by the fishermen who moored their boats in the bay between Houmet Paradis and the Bordeaux headland, and they ran down from this onto the beach, quite puffed out, but still waving madly.

"Oh no! What are we going to do now," said Shani, quite distressed, as *Cobo Alice* disappeared momentarily behind some rocks off the headland. Then by some miracle, so they thought, the boat turned sharply and headed between the rocks, back towards the beach.

Chapter 18

Phil to the Rescue

They ran down to the water's edge as the little boat chugged its way in. Phil, by now, was waving back to them and called out as the boat nosed into the shore.

"What's up?" he said. "I seen you waving all along the top there, and I thought I'd better come in and see what all the fuss is about."

"Oh, Phil," said Anna. "Thank goodness you saw us. Quick, you've got to help us. There're smugglers on the island there, shipwrecked, and they dumped their stuff overboard, just like you said. You know, about pots being hauled up with stuff in them. Please can you help!?"

"Alright, alright," said Phil. "Steady on. Look, now you've got your feet wet. Just hold on a minute while I bring her right in... Okay, I'd better 'ave you lot onboard. Then you can tell me all about it. Shipwrecked you say? Dear oh dear. Come on then, up you come. Just grab my arm."

Phil lifted them up one by one into the boat, and sat them down. He reversed out, then spun the wheel over, to head back the same way he had come in.

"No, they're over there," said Anna. "Back that way, Phil."

"Can't go that way, miss," said Phil. "There's only one way in and out, unless you want to get us shipwrecked too. Now, who are these young gents?"

Anna and Shani introduced Tom, Bart and Ian, and Phil shook hands with them. "Nice to have you on board," he said. "I might be needing three strong lads to help me deal with these smugglers."

As they headed out and turned back again towards the island, the boys explained to Phil exactly what had happened: how they had seen the RIB approaching from around the north of Herm, and narrowly missing the rocks on the way in, and then how the men had dropped the box over the side, and then driven off at full speed and hit the rock.

"Sounds like a bunch of cowboys to me," said Phil. "Now when we get to them, and that'll be in a few minutes with the tide behind us, you let me do the talking."

Cobo Alice fairly shot across the bay, and then turned in behind the lee of Houmet Paradis, where they found the smugglers, sitting on a beach with the RIB pulled in tight against the shore, and the huge outboard motor tilted up out of the water.

The smugglers had planned to lie low until the tide dropped, and then wade across onto the mainland. They had watched the little red white and blue fishing boat go past, and were relieved that they had not been spotted so close to where they had dropped off the box.

At first they thought the damage to their boat was just a broken propeller, but when they removed it they could see that the gearbox casing was cracked and leaking oil.

"We've 'ad it mate," said one of the smugglers. "I don't see 'ow we're going to get outa this."

"I thought you said you knew the rocks around 'ere," said the other. "This is a fine ******* mess you've got us into."

The first smuggler lit up a cigarette, stood up and looked furtively about. "Ere, shut up and listen, you moany old git. There's another boat coming."

Sure enough, they could hear the chugging sound of an engine.

"Get down, you silly sod!" said the other smuggler.

The two of them crouched down alongside the RIB, and anyone simply passing by, who had not seen them arrive, would probably not have noticed them. The black wetsuits and the black RIB were hardly visible against the black rocks. But the crew of *Cobo Alice* knew very well that the smugglers were there, and the little fishing boat swung in towards them.

The second smuggler swore violently. "Right. You just shut up. Don't say a ****** word. I'll 'andle this," he said.

Phil took his boat to within a few yards of the stricken RIB, and then put her into reverse to stop her. "I see you've a problem with your engine," he said. "Can I give you a tow back to St Peter Port?"

"Nah, mate," said the smuggler. "We can manage tah."

"Are you sure about that?" said Phil. "Looks like you've got oil leaking out from somewhere."

A rainbow coloured film of oil was spreading out over the water, all around the RIB, for all to see.

"Nah, mate. We can fix it," said the smuggler. He just wanted to get rid of this nosey fisherman, and all these kids staring at him. This was just what he didn't need.

The explorers didn't like the look of these men at all. One of them was incredibly shifty, the man from the old ruined fort, and the other, who was doing all the talking, had a cruel look about him, with eyes that were dark, dull and evil, as if he had no soul, and not one shred of goodness in him.

"Well, look," said Phil. "I'm just going to radio St Peter Port and let them know you're in trouble. What's your registration number?" He read out the number painted on the stern of the RIB. "Four, five, six, zero. Is that it?"

To have Phil radio St Peter Port was the last thing the smugglers wanted.

"Well, er, maybe you might as well give us a tow, mate. Er, no need to use the radio. Yeah, a tow would be alright. Just chuck us a rope eh?"

The explorers were amazed at Phil's performance. Not once had he even glanced in the direction of the bobber where the box had been sent down, nor had his voice betrayed any sense of anxiety. He had been his usual calm and friendly self, totally matter of fact, and the smugglers had played right into his hands.

Phil was sure now that smugglers they were, but he was careful not to let them see or think for one moment that he knew. He took a length of rope, tied one end to a stern post, coiled it and threw the other end to the smugglers, who made it fast to the towing eye of the RIB. The smugglers climbed on board and pushed the rib out from the shore. *Cobo Alice* took up the strain on the towrope, and then they were off, around the island and out into the passage heading for St Peter Port.

The explorers had kept very quiet while Phil had been dealing with the smugglers, especially Bart, Anna and Shani, who had tried to look the other way, so they would not be recognised. Now, with the chug of the engine to cover their voices, and the splashing of the wake around *Cobo Alice* and her prize, they felt able to speak again.

"What are we going to do now, Phil," whispered Anna, as loud as she dared. "Do you think they really are smuggler? Are they going to be arrested?"

"I,ve been wondering about those two for quite some time," said Phil, in a low voice. "Been flashing their cash around the pubs, fancy boat and all, you don't earn that sort of money out of fishing. We'll have to get them arrested somehow, then we'll find out what's in that box." He paused for a moment and thought about it. "This is going to be tricky," he said. "We've got to radio St Peter Port, but if I pick up that handset they'll see me do it. Then God knows what they would do." He paused again. "Right, got it. Here's what we'll do. One of you will have to get down on the floor and use the radio. I'll tell you what to say. Now you just chat amongst yourselves and look like you're having a nice 'appy day out."

With this, Phil laughed and slapped his thigh, and looked back at the smugglers with a jolly smile.

"So who's it going to be, kids? I think maybe Bart should do it."

Bart nodded. "I'll do my best," he said.

"Right. Now, Tom and Ian, you go up forrard and have a chat, and point at things over the bow," said Phil. "And you two girls come and sit here by me, and we'll have a joke and a laugh. That's right."

Anna and Shani made various actions and mimes, as if they were telling a story, and together with Phil they provided a perfect screen to hide Bart, who now sat in front of them and took the handset of the VHF radio.

"Just press that button when you speak into it," said Phil. "No, hang on. First turn down that volume switch. We don't want them to hear St Peter Port answering us. Now press that button and say after me, St Peter Port, St Peter Port, this is *Cobo Alice*, *Cobo Alice*, over."

Bart repeated the words exactly.

The radio crackled, and a voice came through in reply: "*Cobo Alice*, this is St Peter Port, receiving you, Phil. Can you speak up a bit, I can hardly hear you. Over."

"Now, those smugglers are watching me," said Phil, hardly moving his lips. "You'll have to tell them in your own words, Bart. We need the police down at the old

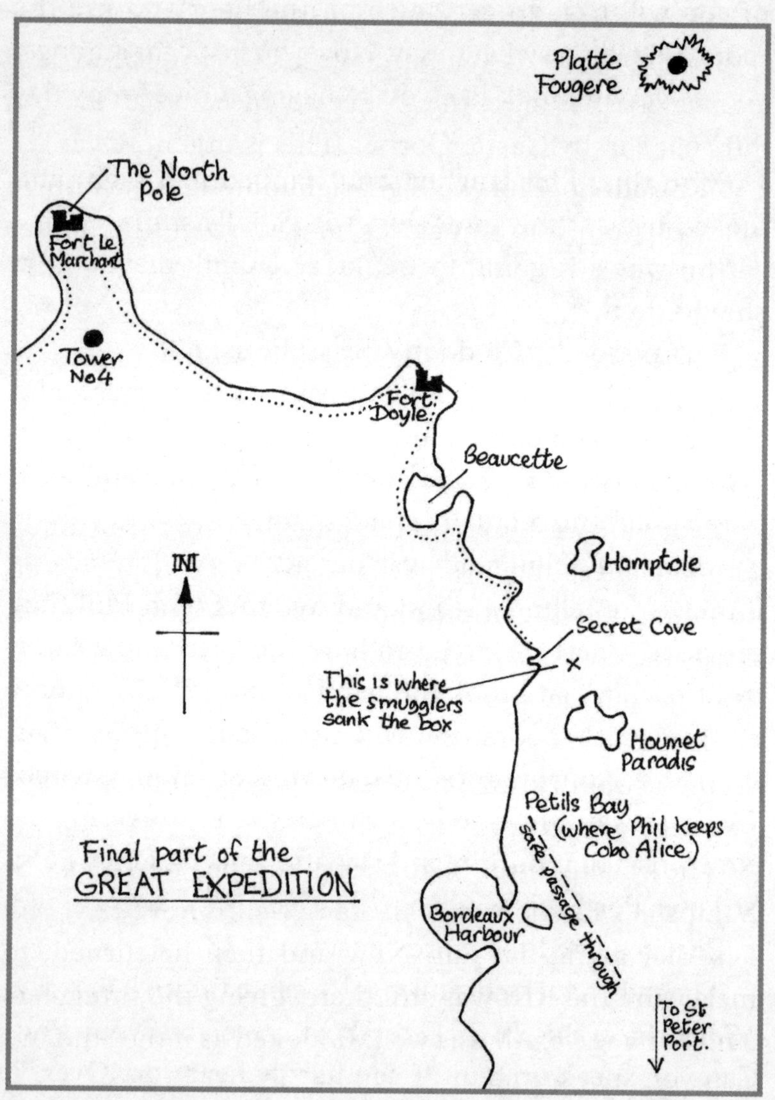
Platte
Fougere
The North
Pole
Fort le
Marchant
Tower
No4
Fort
Doyle
Beaucette
Homptole
N
Secret Cove
This is where
the smugglers
sank the box
Houmet
Paradis
Petils Bay
(where Phil keeps
Cobo Alice)
Final part of the
GREAT EXPEDITION
safe passage through
Bordeaux
Harbour
To St
Peter
Port.

lifeboat slip, by Castle Cornet."

Bart pushed the button down. "St Peter Port, St Peter Port. Sorry can't explain. We are bringing in two smugglers. We need the police to meet us at the old lifeboat slip by Castle Cornet. This is urgent. Over."

"Er right ho, Phil. We'll get right onto it. Just confirm that will you. Two smugglers, and you want the police at the old lifeboat slip. Is that it? Over."

"Affirmative. These men could be dangerous. Please get the police. We'll be there in about fifteen minutes. Over and out."

Phil nodded. "Well done, Bart," he said. "That should do the trick."

Everyone was quiet for a minute or two. In any other circumstances they would have enjoyed a trip like this so much, but the atmosphere onboard *Cobo Alice* was tense, there was no enjoyment to be had. They continued to mime and act as if they were having fun, but in truth they were just longing to get to the safety of the harbour, so they could rid themselves of these awful smugglers and get back to normal.

The valiant little boat was doing her best. Past St Sampson's Harbour and all along Belle Greve Bay, Phil kept her going flat out. Now and then he turned, to make sure the RIB was still there, giving the smugglers a nod or a wave. All was well. It looked as if they did not suspect anything.

As Bart had estimated, the journey to St Peter Port harbour took them about fifteen minutes, but it seemed like hours, then, just as they were approaching the harbour mouth, they heard the sirens. Nothing too unusual about that, thought the smugglers. Could be an ambulance, or a fire engine, or someone caught for speeding. Still, they scanned the seafront, looking to see what all that commotion was about.

Boats entering the harbour normally slow down, but Phil carried on flat out through the pierheads. Ahead of them they saw the old lifeboat slipway, with police vans and cars with flashing lights arriving on the scene.

"Oh no. That's torn it," said Phil. He looked back at the smugglers. The evil looking one was going mad, shouting and swearing and shaking his fist.

"You *******!!!" he screamed. "You wait till I get hold of you!"

Then they were both struggling to undo the towrope, but it was pulled so tight they had no chance.

"Phil!" shouted Anna. "He's got a knife!"

They looked around to see the evil one, with knife in hand, desperately sawing at the towrope. But it was too late. Phil swung *Cobo Alice* expertly around, in and up against the slipway. The RIB swung around in a graceful arc behind them and sailed up the slipway right into the hands of the waiting policemen.

"Drop that knife!" ordered the police sergeant. "Or you'll be in even deeper trouble than you are already."

The smuggler growled and spat in the water, but he could see the game was up. He turned to Phil. "Don't think you can hide from me," he said menacingly. "I'll find out where you live."

Phil looked him straight in the eye. "You can do what

you like," he said calmly. "I don't scare that easy."

The smugglers were handcuffed and led away to the waiting police van. One of the policemen, and a police woman, stayed behind to talk to Phil and his crew.

"We'll be needing statements from all of you, I'm afraid," said the policeman. "Probably best if you come up to the station. Is there anybody you would like us to contact, to let them know what's happened?"

"You'd better phone my mother," said Anna, "Although she'll probably panic."

"Don't worry," said the police woman. "We'll explain you're all safe and well, and she can come and collect you from the station. Now what about the rest of you?"

Names and phone numbers were given, Phil tied up *Cobo Alice* securely to the quay, and the RIB was taken away by the police for further investigation. More police cars arrived to take everyone to the police station, and by this time a large crowd of onlookers had miraculously appeared at the top of the slipway. Even more miraculously, they seemed to know already what had happened.

"Those are the children that caught the smugglers!" a lady called out, as they fought their way through.

"Hurray!" shouted the crowd.

"Aren't they brave!" said another lady, "And they're only young."

"Well done, love!"

"Oh, poor little mites!"

Bart managed to stay calm. Tom and Ian quite enjoyed the attention, but after all that had happened, and now with this outpouring of love and support from the crowd, it was all too much for Shani, who suddenly burst into tears, and then so did Anna.

The police woman was very kind, and did her best to comfort them. “Don’t worry,” she said. “It’s perfectly normal. It’s the shock, you see. It’s just the tension being released.” She handed out some tissues. “Here now, dry your eyes, and don’t be too sad. I shouldn’t be surprised if you get some kind of reward for this! One thing’s for sure: you’re going to be in all of the papers. You’re going to be famous!”

Epilogue

The policewoman was right. The very next day, and for days after, the story of how five children (and a fisherman) had captured the smugglers, appeared in all of the local newspapers, and even some of the nationals.

On finding out that the Riley family were regular visitors to the island, the Guernsey Tourist Board offered for Mr and Mrs Riley, Anna and Shani to have three weeks holiday in Guernsey the following year, all expenses paid.

One of the local chandleries presented Tom, Ian and Bart with vouchers, which they reckoned would cover their boating costs for quite a few years, and buy them some fishing tackle as well.

Although there just was not enough time for all of the explorers to visit the Dehus Dolmen, Tom and Ian went there after all the fuss had died down. They wrote a letter to Anna and Shani, to tell them all about it:

Dear Anna and Shani,

Tom and I thought we should write and tell you about our visit to the Dehus Dolmen. We went on our bikes yesterday.

It wasn't what we were expecting at all. From the outside it looks more like a great big igloo, except there's grass all over the top instead of snow, and there's a path all the way round it. Also there is a little black door with notices all over it and a padlock. We thought it was locked when we got there, but one of the notices said it's open during the hours of daylight, and the light switch is just inside the door. We weren't expecting a light switch! Another notice tells you all about who discovered it and its history since then. We don't need to tell you, as you have this information already in the dolmen book.

Inside it is amazing! There are about 5 or 6 rooms, and we found the carving of the Gardien du Tombeau (I think that's how it is spelt!). It's on the ceiling in the biggest room. We couldn't find it at first, but there is a special light switch that changes the lighting so you can see it better. We thought it was really good, especially his face which has eyes, nose and mouth, and everything.

Anyway, we won't tell you too much about it, as we are sure you will want to have a look for yourselves. It is such a shame we couldn't all be there together to see it, but at least we can now say the final leg of our expedition has been completed, in a way. We are so looking forward to seeing you next year!

We are going to write to Bart. Well, Tom is going to write that one, and I will keep interrupting him, just like he is interrupting me at the moment.

Sorry about that! Just broke off for a bit of wrestling! Which I won. (No he didn't, signed, Tom).

Where were we? Yes. We aren't sure if Bart is back in England yet. Have you heard from him? Tell him we are keeping an eye on the *Esperance* if he phones.

Phil is taking us out fishing next week and we are really looking forward to that. We can try out some of our new fishing tackle.

We've been out a couple of times in *Kitty*, but the weather hasn't been too brilliant for sailing. We could really do with Bart to give us a few more tips.

Anyway, that's about all for now.

Oh no it isn't! Tom has just reminded me. We have thought of a brilliant new name for us. Much better than "Explorers of the Bay." If you think about it, we've gone much further than just around the bay, and we've discovered the Secret Islands, and Guernsey is an Island too, so we thought we should call ourselves "The Islanders." What do you think? Please phone or write and let us know.

Blimey this is a long letter. Really must go now.

Your fellow explorers
Ian Tom

Anna replied as follows:

Dear Ian and Tom

Thank you so much for the lovely letter.

We were pleased to hear you had made it to the Dehus. I can't wait to check it out for myself. It sounds awesome!

Sadly, I don't see any chance of us getting back until next summer, although I am trying my best to work on the parents. Of course now we are back, it is boring old work as usual for Father, homework for Shani and me, and Mother has also settled into her usual routine, which allows very little room for adventure.

The good thing is, we know for sure we will be back in Guernsey next year, because it's already booked and paid for by the very kind people at the Guernsey Tourist Board!

Great to hear you are writing to Bart. He phoned us last week from France. He was having a wonderful time with his father, sailing on some yacht, but I think he's missing us all the same.

Also great to hear about Phil, except we are so envious that you are going out in *Cobo Alice*. We love that boat. Hope Phil will take us out next year!

Your idea that we should be called the Islanders is perfect. Shani and I would love to be Islanders. I've thought up a design for a new flag (see enclosed). What do you think? Maybe you can get one ready for when we next meet up.

Better finish off now. Have to get on with homework. Yuck!

Write again soon!

Lots of love
Your fellow Islanders
Anna and Shani(pp)

PS. Shani wasn't here to sign the letter, but I read it out to her over the phone, and she sends her love and agreed I could sign for her. We'll write the next letter together, so you can be sure it will be longer than this one!

Glossary

Vineries

Guernsey was once famous for its early crops of fruit and flowers. The Channel Islands are the furthest south of all the British Isles, so that daffodils and other spring flowers from Guernsey were often the first on the markets. By growing in glasshouses crops could be produced even earlier. The first crops to be grown under glass were grapes. This is why groups of glasshouses are still called vineries (after the grape vines). Gradually, produce has become available from other parts of the world where it can be obtained virtually all year round at low cost. Most Guernsey growers have found it impossible to compete and sadly many of the vineries have fallen into disrepair, or have been demolished.

Guernsey

Guernsey is the second largest of the Channel Islands, situated some 70 odd miles from the south coast of England, in the bay of St Malo. The island is approximately 9 miles long by 5 miles wide, with a population of approx 60,000.

Guernsey was originally part of Normandy. After the Norman conquest in 1066, when William, Duke of

Normandy, became King of England, the Channel Islands became attached to Britain, and have remained loyal to the British Crown ever since.

Guernseys, as worn by Mr Mahy, are fishermen's sweaters made of oiled wool and traditionally dark blue in colour. They are hard wearing, and highly suitable for fishing and other outdoor pursuits.

Braye du Valle

The Rousse headland forms the southern arm of Grande Havre, which, as the name implies, is a large sheltered bay providing a safe anchorage for a good many fishing and pleasure boats. Along the north and east sides of the bay are a number of sandy beaches, perfect for sunbathing and swimming. Originally, Grande Havre formed the mouth of a seawater channel called the Braye du Valle. This channel separated the Vale from the rest of Guernsey. During the Napoleonic wars it was feared that the French might invade the Vale and then take over the rest of Guernsey, so the channel was filled in. The only remaining parts are Grande Havre at one end, and the Vale Pond just inland of the bay, and at the other end: the Bridge, and St Sampson's Harbour. Many place names reflect the history of the area: the Saltpans, Route Militaire etc.

Herm

Herm Island is about 3 miles off the east coast of Guernsey. One and a half miles long with a population of perhaps a few hundred in the summer, Herm is more fully described in chapter 7.

Gache

Guersey gache is a lightly spiced fruit loaf made with sultanas and/or raisins and currants. Some versions also have candied peel. Recipes have been handed down through generations, and in some cases special methods and ingredients are kept secret. A good slice of buttered Guernsey gache is a heavenly experience, highly recommended by the author.

Linen press

An essential piece of furniture in any Guernsey farmhouse. As the name implies, linen presses were made locally in the 18th and 19th century to hold the household linen. Approx. 7ft high by 4ft wide, with a pair of doors for the upper section and drawers underneath.

Ormers

Ormers are found mainly in the Channel Islands and are considered by many local people to be a great delicacy. In order to protect stocks, ormers may only be taken by shore gatherers at certain low spring tides throughout the year. No diving is allowed and only ormers of a certain size may be taken. On these ormering tides, you will see many enthusiastic ormerers, armed with ormering hooks (a steel rod bent over at one end) inevitably soaked to the skin (wetsuits are not allowed either), wading about the low tide mark in fanatical pursuit of the elusive mollusc.

Model yacht pond

Guernsey is blessed with a sizeable pond, approx 100 x 50 yards, on the emplacement by Castle Cornet. It is a popular place for enthusiasts of all ages to test their model boats, power and sail, radio controlled or otherwise.

RIB

Rigid inflatable boat. High speed craft usually less than 8 metres in length with glass fibre hull and inflatable sponsons. As used by inshore rescue teams.

Dielette

French port, closest to Guernsey, situated approx 27 miles away on the south coast of the Contentin Peninsula. Cherbourg is on the other side of the peninsula, facing north.

Little Russel

The channel between Guernsey and the offshore islands of Herm and Jethou, forming the approach to St Peter Port harbour.